THE PENGUIN CONTEMPORARY AMERICAN FICTION SERIES

LISTENING TO BILLIE

Alice Adams was born in Fredericksburg, Virginia, and educated at Radcliffe College. A distinguished novelist and short-story writer, she has been represented in the annual O. Henry anthology of the best short stories of the year on ten occasions. Her books include the novels *Rich Rewards*, *Families and Survivors* (both published by Penguin Books), and *Careless Love*, as well as the story collections *Beautiful Girl* and *To See You Again* (also published by Penguin). She lives in San Francisco, California.

Listening to Billie

by ALICE ADAMS

Penguin Books

PENGUIN BOOKS

Viking Penguin Inc., 40 West 23rd Street,
New York, New York 10010, U.S.A.
Penguin Books Ltd, Harmondsworth, Middlesex, England
Penguin Books Australia Ltd, Ringwood, Victoria, Australia
Penguin Books Canada Limited, 2801 John Street,
Markham, Ontario, Canada L3R 1B4
Penguin Books (N.Z.) Ltd, 182–190 Wairau Road,
Auckland 10, New Zealand

First published in the United States of America by
Alfred A. Knopf, Inc., 1978
First published in Canada by Random House of Canada 1978
Published by Viking Penguin Inc. 1984

LIBRARY OF CONGRESS CATALOGING IN PUBLICATION DATA
Adams, Alice, 1926—
    Listening to Billie.
    I. Title.
[PS3551.D324L5   1984]   813′.54   84-6432
ISBN 0 14 00.7376 0

Printed in the United States of America by
R. R. Donnelley & Sons Company, Harrisonburg, Virginia
Set in Janson

Page 217 constitutes an extension of this copyright page.

For Victoria Wilson
with love

Listening to Billie

1 / Billie, Alive

Billie is late—of course, she is always late—but the crowd in this small packed room is not resigned: people are restless, and tense. There is a lot of lighting of cigarettes, looking at watches, loud orders for more drinks. And there are scattered rumors: she's sick, she's not coming, been in a wreck—she's just phoned to say she'll be there in ten minutes. And eerily, throughout all that waiting for Billie, on the huge and garish jukebox one of her records is playing; from out of all that poison-colored neon tubing Billie's beautiful, rich and lonely voice is singing, "I cover the waterfront, I'm watching the sea—"

And then suddenly she is there, and everybody knows, and they crane their heads backward to see her, since she has come in by the street entrance like anyone else. Or, not like anyone else at all: she is more beautiful, more shining, holding her face forward like a flower, bright-eyed and smiling, high yellow cheekbones, white teeth and cream-white gardenia at her ear. She is wearing a big fur coat, and behind her is a slouch-hatted man with a huge dog, a Dane, that is straining on a leash. The man has a bandage on his hand: he is Billie's manager, and the dog, Billie's dog, bit him on the hand on the way to the show, and that is why they are late.

With a wonderful gesture Billie throws her coat down on the stage, and for a moment she stands there in the spotlight, mouthing the words that are coming from the jukebox—"Will the one I love, be coming back to me?"—as everyone laughs and screams and applauds.

Somewhere in that audience, probably up near the front, is a very young and pretty small girl, who is not paying much attention to Billie. Eliza Hamilton, with long smooth blond hair that curls suddenly at the ends, and dark blue eyes. She has serious and obsessive problems of her own: is she pregnant? Her heavy breasts are heavier, and sore. And if she is pregnant, what should she do? Should she marry Evan Quarles, the paler blond and sad, Deep Southern young man at her right? He would like them to marry, and that is strange: Eliza knows that she is more in love than he is, but it is he who urges marriage. He is deeply disturbing, mysterious to her; she is both excited and obscurely alarmed by Evan—is that "in love"? He wants them to marry. He has a teaching job for next fall at a small boys' school. Raleigh, in New Hampshire. Now she looks at Evan with a mixture of enmity and curiosity: who *is* he?

Eliza is barely listening to Billie, who now, with her small combo in the background, is singing, "Once they called it jazztime, to a buck and wing—"

Singing, swinging it out.

But Eliza retained that scene of Billie's entrance, and Billie singing. (Singing what? What was she wearing?) She kept it somewhere in her mind; she brought it out and stared at it as she might a stone, something opalescent. At times she wondered how much of it she had imagined. She was a somewhat literary girl, who occasionally wrote poems, although she never finished them, and she did not take this occupation seriously, not yet. For one thing, she felt that she was not the right shape for a poet; a poet, a woman poet, should be tall and thin, like her mother, Josephine, who was a successful writer—powerful, impressive, really formidable—but not a poet. I am too small and round to be a poet, Eliza thought, and of that she thought, Ridiculous!

. . .

Should she have an abortion? Who would know a doctor who would do it? Who would pay for it? Not Evan, and certainly not Josephine; she could never even tell Josephine.

But even in the midst of such frenzied speculations, Eliza is aware that this evening—these hours—are important; she *knows* she will remember. And she thinks of the following Monday, when she will be back in Connecticut, in school, and she will tell her friends about seeing Billie—how beautiful she was, her voice. How Evan Quarles, the interesting older man, took her to Fifty-second Street to hear Billie Holiday. She will not tell any friend that she might be pregnant.

Billie has stopped singing, left the stage, and Evan says, "I'd buy you a gardenia if I weren't allergic to them." He laughs ambiguously, and he waves away the haggard, spike-lashed woman with the tray of corsages—gardenias, wilting rosebuds. "You haven't finished your drink," he says. "Drink up. God knows they're weak enough."

Will he want to make love later? Will he take her back to his place, on Horatio Street, in the Village? Eliza can't be sure of anything with Evan. She gulps at her drink obediently.

Evan gestures that the room is too noisy for conversation. True enough, but is he not having a good time?

Eliza looks around at all the other talking people, and she suddenly perceives, feels, that there is an extraordinary number of handsome young men, all strangers, all unexplored and possible. She looks at them intently, the gray flannel suits or tweed coats, the young male faces, some still with summer tans—and so *attractive*, all of them. Aware of her own look, its intentness, she wonders what message she is delivering: is she somehow inviting them, or saying goodbye, as she would to other men if she should marry? And if she should not be pregnant, will she meet one of these new young men months later, and together will they remember hearing, seeing Billie? Will that happen?

Then Eliza notices that the young woman at the next table is heavily pregnant, so huge she must sit back in her chair. Eliza's spirits sink, her fantasy vanishes. She recognizes that young woman as an omen, a terrible sign: she, Eliza, *is* pregnant.

Most of Evan's friends lived near him in the Village, around Abingdon Square, West Fourteenth Street. Young men recently down from Harvard or Yale—a few from Princeton, Evan's school. Some had graduated, a surprising number had been expelled—it was never quite clear for what.

They worked in publishing, or on magazines. They were all vaguely "literary." They "wrote." All except Evan, who wanted to give up all that; he was serious about teaching. They were fond of Twenties' fiction, Thirties' poets. Firbank and Fitzgerald, Auden and Isherwood and Spender. They were also fond of veiled jokes about "boys who like boys," and their code words for that condition, thanks to Senator McCarthy, were "Security Risk." "Do you think he could be a Security Risk?" "Well, it's not unlikely." Discreet laughter.

All, to Eliza, heady and hyper-sophisticated stuff.

Some of them even smoked marijuana, then called "tea." Evan didn't like it. "I'll stick to my proved old bourbon." Heavy drinking was also new to Eliza. She and Evan always were a little drunk when they made love.

Evan wanted to get away from his friends. Eliza understood that they made him nervous. He wanted to make a new life in the New England countryside. With her.

Now Billie is walking back onto the stage; amid thundering applause, shouts and whistles, she saunters into the smoke-beamed center of light; she stands there, one hip thrust forward. She scans the crowd as though she could see everyone there. Is she possibly seeing the men and feeling the urgent attraction that

Eliza felt a few minutes before? Her eyes are blank, and her smile says nothing.

"She looks bad," Evan whispers—too loudly, Eliza feels, even in that noisy room. "Drugs—she can't last long."

"Georgia, Georgia, no peace I find . . ." sings Billie, whose beautiful face has come alive, whose eyes say everything.

Married to Evan, and pregnant, Eliza sometimes played Billie's records, always remembering her face and the creamy velvet flower in her hair.

Evan was excessively busy; he took his teaching and his students with a passionate seriousness. He seemed to believe that sex was bad for pregnant women. Eliza felt heavily distasteful to herself, as well as to Evan.

When their child was born, a fat blond girl whom they named Catherine, Eliza knew that she was no longer "in love" with Evan, but perhaps that had been replaced by motherhood? In any case she loved her daughter very much. Having vaguely felt that her own mother, successful Josephine, was unmaternal (did Josephine ever feed her? Eliza could only remember maids), Eliza concentrated on feeding and loving Catherine.

Perhaps forgetting Evan?

One bright fall day at lunch, in his soft Southern voice, Evan announced, "The most beautiful boy in the world has appeared in my Cicero class."

Eliza was feeding Catherine in her highchair. "Really?" she said. She was distracted, spooning mashed plums into Catherine's purple mouth.

"Really. He's enough to make me wonder if I could be queer. A Security Risk." Saying this, Evan laughed unsuccessfully, ending in a cough. He had gained a lot of weight in the past couple of years. He was drinking too much.

Eliza was unpleasantly struck by what he had said, and she thought, perhaps unkindly, that he was not really sophisticated enough to get away with a remark of that sort. Or was he testing her sophistication? Also, since they almost never made love, what he said could only be depressing.

But then, in the following months, as it became clear that Evan was truly, obsessionally in love with that beautiful boy, Eliza experienced a sort of relief: his distaste for her was not her fault; she was not a distasteful person, she was simply a woman.

She was much less shocked by the idea of actual homosexuality than Evan was (it was not the same as jokes about Security Risks), and thus—or so she felt the situation—she was faced with two necessities: one, of comforting Evan, of saying that what he felt was all right (she was not worried about scandal; guilty Evan would not "make a pass" at that beautiful boy, would only follow him around helplessly); and two, of separating herself from him.

Because of Catherine, it was more immediately practical for Evan to move out, and so he did, discreetly, to a local inn, called The Ark—an ancient, looming place, in which both Josephine and Eliza's half-sister, Daria Paulus, had stayed for occasional visits.

Once they were divorced, Eliza planned to move to California.

One night, alone, in The Ark, Evan took an overdose of sleeping pills along with his bourbon.

Seeing his dead face while she was still in shock—just before the rush of namable emotions, the grief and guilt and rage—Eliza first thought, How strange; how happy he looks now.

2 / Eliza's House

With Evan's insurance money, and with a little of her own capital, Eliza was able to buy, at last, a small cottage in San Francisco, on the eastern slope of Russian Hill. A small hilltop house from which enormous views were visible: a sweep of the Bay, Treasure Island and the long Bay Bridge, the hills of Oakland and Berkeley. Boats, and lights and stars. And the situation of the house was perfect, as people were apt to say. Its being on a cul-de-sac insured some privacy and safety—although parking was a considerable problem, which was one of the reasons that Eliza did not own a car. (Others were ideological; she disapproved of their fumes, and the *danger* of cars.)

Her house had the shape of a drawing by a child: square, with a tall chimney and symmetrically slanted roof. Two large rooms upstairs, separated by a hall and a bathroom, and downstairs was the same arrangement: living room, and across the entrance hall a generous kitchen–dining room. Compact, complete.

In the living room there was too much furniture: a lot of smooth bare wood—a carved mantel, salvaged from a wrecking company and lovingly stripped down to its warm mahogany, some small low tables, a rocker. Refinishing furniture was a minor occupation but a major pleasure of Eliza's. She had a sensual feeling for wood, for its smooth unvarnished touch. She even enjoyed the messier aspects of stripping it, the Jasco and steel wool, fine sandpaper and turpentine.

The upholstered things, the big sofa and three club chairs, were soft and somewhat shabby; Eliza, who was *not* handy at upholstery, had attempted to do it herself.

However, the total effect of the house was generous and comfortable, if a little disheveled. It overflowed, literally, with books and records and magazines, usually with music and flowers and good smells of food.

And at that time of her life Eliza's visual effect was rather like that of her house; she, too, often looked a little disheveled, though attractive and comfortable; a generously built small woman. And just as her house beneath its surface mess was clean, so she was fastidious about baths and underclothing, but often wore jeans that were stained with Jasco or olive oil—something—and often old shabby sweaters.

Sometimes a man who was in love with Eliza would feel that the house was too perfect, too complete, as the same man might feel that Eliza as a woman was too independent, that there was no room for him. A man whom she saw sometimes, whom she thought of as The Lawyer, felt an exclusion by the house, and he had no better house to offer Eliza—Eliza and her daughter Catherine. On the other hand, for another man, The Consul, an intense, illicit lover of a few years back—for The Consul's purposes that house was ideal; it suited his dashing arrivals, often for brief visits while taxis waited expensively below. And on the many occasions when it was *impossible* for him to arrive, the thought of Eliza's house assuaged his guilt; there she would be, nevertheless, safe and comfortable in her attractive house, among her records and her books, with her delightful small daughter for company.

During the summer after Billie Holiday died, or killed herself, was killed—one could take any view—after that bad July night (Eliza reacted to the death in a violent, personal way), she did not play Billie's records, but sometimes, with a morbid insistence, they came over the radio, unbidden.

On one such night, that August, Eliza was sitting with a new young man, with whom she had earlier had dinner; he was neither a Lawyer nor a Consul; she was not quite sure what he did. Red-haired, slightly plump, a Boston accent. He had been told to "look up" Eliza by her half-sister, Daria, ten years younger than Eliza, now in school in Boston.

From outside, a mean California summer wind enwrapped the house, its threatening whine clearly audible above the music, above Billie's song. And perhaps for that reason—the wind—otherwise inexplicable tears came close to Eliza's eyes, and she turned to the young man as though he might be of help.

Possibly, probably, later on they would make love; his proprietary hand on Eliza's knee made it clear that he believed that would happen, although as she thought of this, looking at him and even smiling, Eliza realized that she didn't want to—she wished that she were alone. And she discovered in herself some warning, some certain sign of an approaching danger. For one thing, she did not come close to weeping every time she listened to Billie, even now; she was not so sentimental as that. And it had been years since she wept over Evan Quarles.

Catherine was asleep upstairs—Catherine, with whom Eliza had been pregnant as she listened to Billie that night on Fifty-second Street. Thinking of Catherine asleep, Eliza, even with tears in her eyes, considered that her life could be much worse: that bad-sad marriage was over, if dreadfully; her small blond daughter was for the most part a joy. And if she, Eliza, was not doing much—was certainly not doing anything as important as poetry—on the other hand she was coping with her life: her daughter, friends and lovers, the necessary part-time jobs that came her way.

But all in all that evening had been odd, those hours with the new young man. He turned out to be less a friend of Daria's than of someone named "Smith Worthington," whom he, the young man, described to Eliza as Daria's fiancé—although this could not be true; Daria would have told Eliza. The two women, despite the ten years' difference in age, were very close. (Daria was Josephine's child by her third marriage, Eliza by her first.) And the obligatory conversation of two people yoked by an absent third had been curious. Eliza's feelings about her delicate, difficult, sometimes crazily impulsive sister were strong but not readily expressed. (Daria was sometimes crazily generous: Eliza could hear her thin voice saying to an almost stranger, "Oh, you're going to San Francisco? Well, you must look up my sister Eliza Quarles.") How could she talk about Daria to this Bostonian stranger, who was using a pompous word like "fiancé" and an improbable name, "Smith Worthington"? Of his own name, she had all evening been unsure. Bill?

He was curiously monochromatic, that "Bill"; he was all the same pale shade of red. Was that his name, then—Red, not Bill? Very likely his body hair would be the same color—and that decided Eliza: no, she would not make love to anyone with a mat of red hair on his chest. What was odd was that she had even thought that she would, that she *could*. And then she saw what it was strange that she had not seen before: she had for several years been forcing love, or, rather, sex.

After Evan's death and her move to California, although she met a lot of people, men who took her out, for a while she was obstinately celibate. Even when a man appealed to her, she would turn him down, and later go to bed alone and wonder why; surely no one else would turn out to be like Evan? And then came the period that perhaps just then was ending, a time during which if she liked a man at all or if he seemed to expect it, she would go to bed with him. But not that night. Not Red.

Red began, just then, determinedly to kiss her, grasping and pressing and pulling, as Eliza resisted him, almost absent-mindedly, still thinking.

Then he muttered, "Come on, baby, you know you want it, too," in an accent quite unlike the one he had been using earlier—tough, threatening, street vowels.

At which she was mobilized, "Get out—go away," she

managed to say, pulling back from him—as, ghoulishly, on the radio Billie began to sing, "I've got a right to sing the blues, I've got a right to moan and sigh . . ."

He didn't believe her; or he thought that her struggle was a come-on? That she was being coy?

Anyhow, the struggle went on and on; it was purely and simply a fight, the sex had gone out of it. And so, at last, when Eliza said, "Okay, you're stronger than I am, you've proved that," and lay back on her sofa, submissive, actually she had won.

"Well, *shit*." Bill, or Red, pulled himself together, and with what dignity he could find he left.

But could he have been a friend of Daria's? Could Daria have a "fiancé" named Smith Worthington?

Alone, hunched up in her large bed and hearing the louder, more menacing wind, Eliza did not cry, although that was certainly what a part of her would have liked to do; she sensed that somewhere within her there was a woman weeping, or perhaps it was a terrified child, its heart already broken.

3 / In Maine

The next summer, a little over a year after Billie's death, Eliza, perhaps reminded by the music on the record player, tried to describe the night on Fifty-second Street to her sister Daria Paulus, who was only a child that night when Billie sang.

"But *really?* You were there and saw Billie? Alive? How come you've never told me before?"

They were sitting in adjacent white wicker chairs, next to the suspended sofa, both facing the lake, so that from time to time either woman could look out to the water. Not confronted with each other, it was easier for them to talk.

Eliza said, "I thought I had."

"Never. What was she like?" Daria then looked fully at her sister.

"She was beautiful, but it's hard to remember. So many years ago, and I've spent so much time since thinking about her. Listening to her records."

This conversation took place on a late summer afternoon, at one end of the long porch of a large gray-shingled house (Josephine's—their mother's—house); at the other end were a porte-cochère and a parking area.

Daria was thin and dark and delicate. Her long eyes varied from yellow to green to brown to gray; her hair was filmy, black-brown. And Eliza, at almost thirty, looked stronger; her face had more definition than when she was simply a pretty girl. Fine lines had appeared in the corners of her eyes. But she could still be described as small and round. Both young women resembled their fathers: Caleb Hamilton, who, like Evan Quarles, committed suicide, after the stock market crash in 1929, before Eliza was born—a ghastly coincidence, whatever one chooses to call it, which has never been discussed as such between mother and daughter; and Jason Paulus, Daria's father, referred to by Josephine (tactlessly, in Daria's view) as "that Greek shit, but terribly good-looking."

The two women sat tensely forward; they were smoking a lot and drinking iced tea. Below the porch, a flat, well-tended lawn stretched forward to a narrow white beach of rough sand—to the lake. Now the dark water was smooth, barely lapping at the shore, and in the green-white leaves of the clumps of birches there was hardly a stir. Later, in the cool, brisk fall, there would be brilliant, wind-torn days, when the lake was churned with waves into whitecaps, like a small and troubled sea, and the birches bent down with wind. But now the whole scene was quiescent, at peace, and the distant mountain peaks were obscured in a golden haze.

Daria was to be married the next day to the man named Smith Worthington; it was true what Red-Bill had told Eliza, in San Francisco, last summer. And the small family—Josephine and her two daughters, and Eliza's daughter, Catherine—had assembled itself for the wedding.

Daria, still preoccupied with the fact of Eliza's having actually *seen* Billie Holiday, asked her sister, "I wonder why the dog bit the man's hand, her manager. Were they married, or was he her lover?" Billie's beauty, and the dog and the bitten hand were the only details that Eliza had been able to remember, so far.

"I don't know, at all," Eliza answered, musingly. "Sometimes I wonder if I saw another man, somewhere else, with a dog on a leash and a bandaged hand. Maybe Billie came in late, all by herself. Of course that's what I remember best. Her face."

Then, having said all that, Eliza suddenly wondered *why* they were talking about Billie so much, or why at all, when tomorrow Daria was going to marry Smith, a promising young man, if a little colorless—in both respects a contrast to Daria's usual friends (Eliza's, too), who have been, in Josephine's phrase, "more than a little odd": shy, anxious, difficult boys, usually very poor. Why were they not talking about Smith, the wedding, their future as a couple?

Daria's wedding was to be, romantically, in the orchard in back of the house. The orchard of gnarled apple trees, with their thick green leaves—a space crossed with low gray stone fences and bordered by dark woods of pine and fir and hemlock. Farther within those woods were huge boulders, dislodged in some ancient Ice Age, now submerged in roots and overgrown with underbrush, scattered with pine needles, almost camouflaged.

The wedding was planned by Josephine—the successful writer, but not a poet: some essays, biography, travel. A couple of early short stories. Liking to be in charge, Josephine was good at plans.

"Or did she ever marry anyone?" asked Daria, still speaking of Billie. And then in a softer voice she asked, "Was Evan with you when you saw her?"

Intimacy between the two sisters had been uneven, partly because of the difference in age; not, Eliza thought, because of separate fathers. Eliza had seen their friendship as marked with dark areas of reticence, like craters, or whatever they are, on the moon. But, she wondered, does there come a time when all areas should be explored, illuminated? Should she then say: Evan and I weren't getting along, and then he fell in love with someone else, someone forbidden?

Daria's thin face was sharpened and flushed with intensity; her eyes were gray and luminous.

Gently, Eliza said, "Yes, I was with Evan. Not long before we were married." And lightly she added, "Billie was one of the few things we agreed on. We were both crazy about her."

"Smith and I like Billie, too," said Daria, and then added, with one of her infrequent jolts of humor, "I hope that's not a bad sign?"

With a sort of relief both women laughed; they lit new cigarettes and concentrated on their tea, in which most of the ice had melted.

"Or," said Daria, "is it a bad sign that Smith and Josephine are so uneasy with each other?" At times Daria's voice was curiously old; it became tight and dry.

Eliza reassured her, "Not really. I think it's the idea of husbands. Evan, and her own three. Marriage itself."

Then Daria asked, "What about Billie—did she always support herself? I wonder how much money she earned."

And that question was understood by Eliza as an oblique reference to and question about Smith, an economist, who presumably was interested in money, and who would probably earn a lot. Eliza had understood several things at once: Daria was purposefully not talking about Smith, and her marriage to him—perhaps out of nervousness, reasonable in any wedding circumstances, Eliza thought. And also Daria was wondering about Eliza's marriage to Evan. What really happened? why were they getting a divorce? why did Evan kill himself?

"I don't know," Eliza said, of Billie and money. "I don't think money was exactly her thing, somehow." She was unable not to say this defiantly, money not being her thing either. Then, afraid as always of having too great an influence on her sister, and of sounding opposed to Smith, she modified: "I think she was pretty careless about money."

And she wondered: did she say that for Smith's indirect approval? She had so far very little sense of Smith. He had a kind of anonymous pleasantness, but he smoked a pipe, and Eliza had a vague prejudice against pipe-smokers.

"In any case, there they are," said Daria, as a car was heard being jolted over bumps, then harshly braked. "Why must she always drive?"

"She doesn't trust anyone else."

. . .

Behind the orchard a narrow road wound into the woods; at the beginning it was pine-needled, passing the hidden boulders and the thickets. Then it became hard, white-surfaced, winding between strict dark Norway pines, past small grassy meadows and an occasional farmhouse. The barns were connected to the houses by closed passageways, against heavy winter weather, and when the barn was larger than the house, it meant the man was in charge, as Josephine had pointed out to Smith in the course of this afternoon's excursion. She had for the first time noticed that in this area most of the houses were larger than the barns—and why? Her practiced writer's mind noted this for possible exploration.

The white road then reached a narrow black asphalt highway, where it ended. The highway returned eventually to the lake, which was glimpsed at intervals between pine woods, or beyond a hillock of grass. There were cemeteries of broken gray or old white stones, a logging camp, then a crossroads with a grocery store and a small library.

Josephine and Smith had traversed all that this afternoon; she had chosen errands as a not terribly original way of getting to know Smith. The "Evan experience," as she thought of it, not to mention her own three marriages—none madly successful, she sometimes sighingly said, at those moments forgetting the adored middle husband: Franz, killed in Spain, by whom she had no child—all that had made her nervous about the marriages of her daughters. Daria at twenty seemed incredibly young, and so vulnerable, much more so than Eliza at that same age. Eliza had always been strong—unlike her father, thought Josephine, remembering Caleb Hamilton. Like both her daughters, Josephine married at twenty.

In the back seat was Catherine, Eliza's daughter. Catherine, fat and blond, pleasantly self-sufficient, affectionate and rather quiet—qualities that were to describe her for life, more or less.

The afternoon had been nice enough, but unsuccessful—Smith had not let himself be known. He was exceptionally polite—though not, thank God, with those elaborate manners Evan had, but then poor Evan was so Southern. And Smith had an air of innocence—that smooth, clear white skin, those wide and opaque brown eyes. But how could a brilliant young economist—Harvard, *summa cum laude,* a Ph.D. at twenty-four—possibly be so innocent? Josephine had tried to draw him out about politics—to her, always crucial in an assessment of people—but with considerable unsuccess. He was unenthusiastic about the Kennedys, as she was herself, but she was unable to tell from which point of view: her own, which was vaguely Marxist, or from the right.

At least his features were not bland: Smith was a decisively handsome young man, with thick dark brown hair above a fine high white forehead, and eyebrows that flared up slightly at the ends. Only his chin was a little blurred. Thinking ahead, Josephine decided that he would look even better in middle age: distinguished, properly graying. Perhaps he would go into politics.

"Have you ever thought about politics for yourself?" she asked.

"Never," said Smith, more firmly than he had said anything so far.

Using an old phrase of her own, Josephine thought, He's a Money Person. (A phrase in which she never saw any irony: to many people, including her daughters, she herself, being a rich woman, could be called a Money Person.)

Josephine had looked the same for the past twenty years: a tall thin woman with very white hair and bright blue eyes, a smoothly tanned skin. Still somewhat Thirties in her behavior, left-wing Thirties with its bohemian overtones, she tended to dress in ways that could be described as peasanty; her daughters so described her longish flowered skirts and billowing blouses. She was aware of that view, but did not care at all; a secure woman, she knew that that was how she liked to dress.

She parked the car in the clearing beyond the porte-cochère, and she and Smith walked around to the porch with Catherine. Daria got up to greet them. Eliza had gone inside to turn the record off.

At dinner, as she sometimes did, Josephine talked more than anyone else, and with an unaccustomed lurch of sympathy Eliza thought: poor Josephine, she's more unstrung than any of us are. The meal was one of Josephine's worst; deeply uninterested in food, except abstractly, Josephine regarded attention paid to cooking as frivolous. Tonight she had underdone both the chicken and the corn.

Eliza, in her mind, was writing a letter to a man with whom she was still involved, The Lawyer. The night with Red-Bill marked the end of "sleeping around"; rather arbitrarily she settled on The Lawyer for monogamy, and although he was dull she sometimes thought of marrying him, in moods in which she thought that she *should* marry. "This house is from another world," she was writing, in her mind. "Certainly another century. Actually my mother inherited it when her parents died, and it has survived all the storms of her life, the husbands and her work, Daria and me. I think she would die if she lost it, and it is a wonderful house. The rooms—the halls—kitchen—the pantry that smells of apples—all the windows looking out to the lake. The attic full of books, and generations of dolls. Dolls' houses." She imagined that after dinner she would go upstairs and write that letter; very likely, Daria and Smith would want to be alone, and Josephine always worked at night. She had said that she was well into a book about Dorothy Thompson, whom she knew and greatly admired.

"It will actually be more like a party than a wedding, a nice informal family party. Just a few neighbors, old friends." Josephine had said all this before, several times, in the course of the day. "Smith, dear, won't you have another ear of corn? Catherine?"

Smith declined; Catherine said, "Yes, I'll have at least two more."

But later, in her room, although seated at her desk, Eliza did not write a letter; she worked on a poem, or perhaps it was a poem. She played with images of the house and the lake, a kaleidoscope of words, of patterns of words—and she smiled to herself with pleasure as she worked.

The night was very warm for Maine, in late August, and just then it was whitely illuminated by the moon; moonlight made long shadows across the lawn, below Eliza's window, and out on the lake there was a glimmering path of moonlight. Once, a long time ago, she and Daria had gone out in a canoe at night to follow such a path: Eliza could see them clearly now, as though from the shore—herself, much taller, paddling in the stern, and small Daria in the bow, putting down her paddle and turning excitedly to exclaim, or to ask something.

Now, on an impulse, Eliza decided to go outside for a moment, to abandon what was not yet a poem, and to see the lake and the moonlight.

It seemed silly to dress again; she left her room and tiptoed down the hall, naked beneath her linen robe. She remembered a childhood time of terror in that hall: she had been reading *Scottish Chiefs,* and imagined that English ghosts lurked there. She passed the room next to hers, in which Catherine was sleeping, passed Josephine's room. Daria and Smith had tactfully been given adjoining rooms at the far end of the hall, in which, Eliza supposed, they were sleeping, or making love.

She went down the wide steps, tiptoeing, guarding against creaks, across the broad entrance hall, and she opened the door to the porch.

Someone was out there, someone sitting on the chair where that afternoon she herself had sat, next to Daria on her chair, as they talked and listened to Billie. A man was there. But before she had time to be frightened, she saw that it was Smith.

Smith Worthington, still fully dressed, with his unlit pipe in one hand.

Irritated, she nevertheless said, softly and pleasantly, "Oh, hi," and—unavoidably—she went over to where he sat.

Oddly enough, he seemed very glad to see her; rising, affably touching her elbow, he said, "How nice. I've been hoping that sometime we could talk."

She sat down docilely in what had been Daria's chair, and she wondered what he could possibly want to talk about—to her. She was conscious of her nakedness beneath the robe, her big loose breasts, and for an instant it occurred to her that Smith would make love to her—or would try. But of course he did not; he was not like that. Nevertheless, she tightened the robe about her and sat up straight, and asked, "Where's Daria?"

"Asleep, I guess." He sounded puzzled, but then seemed quickly to catch what she meant. "Oh, I see. You thought that I—that we—that Daria and I would be together."

It was said accusingly, and so Eliza admitted, "Well, yes, I did think so." Well, yes, she thought that people who loved each other would make love (even—as she had pointed out to Evan-dying-of-guilt—if it broke certain rules).

Now she sighed, knowing surely that their conversation would be impossible.

He surprised her by saying next, "I haven't really told Daria this yet, but there's a good chance that we may move out to California. To your area, in fact."

"Really? But that's marvelous."

"Yes." He paused momentarily, so that again she thought obscurely of sex. Then he said, "There's an opportunity for me to make a great deal of money."

In the half-light, the midnight moonlight, Smith's face was vague, was more boyish, more innocent even than usual. Suppose, Eliza unreasonably wondered, suppose I made a pass at him, reached and knowingly kissed that soft curved mouth? But why did she even think of this, since it was not something that she wanted to do? She looked out at the glinting lake, at the

23

cold gray sand where she had meant to walk, feeling more lonely than if she were in fact alone.

Of course she should have asked Smith about his work possibility, but she did not know what to ask, and she remembered a phrase of Josephine's: the Money People. What Smith was, what she was not.

He surprised her again by saying, "I don't know the San Francisco area well at all. And I was wondering about an appropriate place for us to live."

One of us, Eliza at that moment thought, one of us is crazy. But why should it be Smith, who after all was not saying anything so bizarre? "Appropriate" may be a pompous word, but not a crazy one. And not for the first time she thought, I am the one who is mad, it is obviously me.

"Woodside," she said to Smith. "Daria loves the country, and it's elegant there. It will remind her of here. Of Maine."

He took out a tiny notebook and made a notation. Then he asked Eliza, "How far from the city, would you say?"

"I don't know. Less than an hour's drive, I think."

He noted that also, and then said what perhaps he had meant to say all along: "I do hope, Eliza, that your own life will be more settled. Soon."

She giggled in a way that was girlish and quite out of character. Who was she—Daria? Possibly her daughter Catherine? Then she said, "I suppose you mean that I should get married—again?"

What else could he possibly mean? Smith nodded.

Having judged that he considered her crazy, and that quite possibly he was right, Eliza decided that she would confirm his view; she would make him see her as really mad.

"I'm not really convinced about marrying," she said. "Isn't it perhaps done too often? Look at Josephine. Once might be enough. Really, why should I marry again? Why would marriage make me more *appropriate?*" She was unable not to italicize the word.

"Well, I do see that your first experience was unfortunate,"

Smith managed to say. "But I'm sure next time it will all work out."

She was off. "Unfortunate! Poor Evan, he never should have married anyone, especially not me. But I was pregnant, and he felt guilty about me, we both felt guilty. What a way to marry!" She realized that she was speaking too loudly. She stopped, and in the silence that followed she crazily imagined that a ghostly Billie Holiday was singing; she could hear that solitary mourning voice.

"I didn't know all that," said Smith. Could this possibly be true? Surely everyone knew she was pregnant; even Daria at that age could count.

"There's more," Eliza said wildly; she was on the verge of saying to him what she had not said to anyone in her family, especially not to Daria: Evan fell in love with someone else, a boy.

Now she did not say that to Smith, either; she felt that Smith could handle such information even less than Daria could.

"I'm not even very interested in money," Eliza feebly said, instead. "Why marry?"

He laughed in a small dismissing way. "That's easy for you to say."

Eliza experienced a curious sense of elation: having meant to sound insane, to shock Smith, she felt herself instead coming into focus, as sometimes words did when she was writing.

She stood up. "Well, actually I came down to walk on the beach, but I guess I won't."

He stood, too. He said, "You know, you're really crazy."

"You're probably right."

Eliza had a photographic memory, of a certain kind: certain scenes flashed across her mind like slides. Earlier, talking to Daria, she had *seen* Billie enter the night club on Fifty-second Street, and this short space of time with Smith was another scene that she remembered and reviewed in years to come. But for a long time that moment of elation was missing from the picture; she might as well have been drunk, or high. Nor, remembering Smith's pale serious young face, was she sure what made him think that she was crazy.

The wedding was just as Josephine intended: beautiful and conclusive Episcopal words were spoken, and then it was a party, in an orchard on a brilliant, deep blue afternoon. Fall was somehow suddenly in the air, along with smells of apples and of freshly mown grass, of sweet dry hay, and wind. Goldenrod stood beside the road, and Indian paintbrush, beside the low stone fences. And behind the orchard the long house lay low against the land, its long windows reflecting the lowering sun, its shingles silver in that fading light.

All afternoon Eliza had watched the joyously innocent faces of Daria and Smith. Together they looked even younger than either separately did. And, juxtaposed to Smith's soft face, Daria's features were finer, sharper and more poignant than before.

To Eliza the sight was terribly sad. But after all, there was always the chance that what happened would be unusual—a good marriage. It was she, Eliza, who was crazy, not Smith Worthington.

Fat and happy and pretty in her flowered dress, Catherine, who was the flower girl, loved everything about this wedding. "I love weddings!" she cried out to her mother, to Eliza. "How many times are people allowed to marry? I'd like to be a bride a dozen times."

The other guests were mostly old—old friends of Josephine's, old neighbors. Gently shocked, they now laughed softly at Catherine; they looked curiously at Eliza, never knowing what anyone in this family would say or do.

Josephine was angrily thinking of her third wedding, to Jason Paulus. And at the same time she knew that her rancor was unfair. Jason was not actually a bad person. A Money Person, yes, in real estate, in Westchester—but not actually dishonest. He simply fell in love with Josephine and she forced herself to marry him—not knowing that marriage to Jason would simply exacerbate her pain at Franz's loss. Ah, marriages! she thought, and scowled. But no one noticed.

Eliza took her daughter's hand, and they started toward the house, toward the festively decorated dining room, and the cutting of the cake.

That night, after Daria and Smith and all the wedding guests were gone, Eliza and Josephine sat in the adjacent wicker chairs on the long front porch, watching the flickering lights from the faintly smaller moon as it was reflected in the lake's small waves. The two women, unlikely mother and daughter, secret enemies, or so they seemed to themselves, conversed in a desultory, pleasant, if nearly exhausted way, as they listened to music from the machine inside the house.

Not Billie; they were listening to someone named Horace Silver, whom Eliza had not heard before—a marvelous, dazzling pianist.

"And a Portuguese Negro," explained Josephine. "Satisfying two of my positive biases."

They laughed, and then Eliza said, "Well, yes, but do Portuguese really qualify as a minority?"

"I don't know about that, but some of them are terribly attractive. One almost broke my heart. A consul."

An unusual remark from Josephine, and for an instant they were simply two women, talking. Eliza wished her mother would go on in that vein. She would like to ask when? where? was he married? a Catholic? Well, of course he would have been. She would like to say: I, too, had a lot of trouble with a consul (The Consul). How did you handle it—what happened?

But Josephine had her own ideas about mother-daughter conversations, as she did about most things. "In any case, isn't Horace Silver marvelous?" she said.

"Isn't he, though," agreed her daughter, who was thinking that what he is is incredibly sexy, which she did not say.

The record stopped, and neither woman moved to change it.

And into that silence Josephine made her second startling remark of the evening. She said, "Smith—there's something so very odd about that boy. I don't know—"

"Yes." They looked at each other, another rare moment of accord. But neither of these highly verbal women was able to say what she thought.

"He's very ambiguous," said Josephine, and then laughed, aware that she had echoed what Smith himself said when she questioned him about a certain contemporary political figure, from California—a man who, to Josephine, was an unambiguous villain.

From far across the lake a loon called, and Josephine said, "They always sound somehow female, don't they?"

"Yes."

On the other side of the lake, just visible now in the moonlight, were some small and oddly shaped islands, mostly rocks, with dark clumps of trees. Loons lived there, and other wild birds, and squirrels and chipmunks and rabbits. "Someone told me," said Josephine, "that those islands are very like those along the coast of Yugoslavia, below Dubrovnik." She laughed. "I must be getting ready for a trip."

They were quiet for a while, and then they both said that it was time for bed; they were tired.

At the head of the stairs they lightly kissed good night, and separated.

Seated at her desk, Eliza took up the fragments, the patterns of words that she had begun the night before. She crossed out one that was wrong, added a phrase. What was now on the paper was a mess, and so on a clean page she copied it out. She read over what was there, and her blood raced as she recognized what she saw: a finished poem, small and beautiful, complete.

She got up abruptly from the desk; she hurried to get ready for bed.

Although tired, she was wakeful; her mind raced about, back and forth across her life, those almost thirty years of it. Behind her closed eyelids her past was vividly present: she could see Evan (with diminishing pain, she noted, at last), could see chunky Catherine, as a baby, laughing, Daria, a dark and skimpy little girl, near this house, crying over a kitten that had been scratched by a squirrel—this house that she could see steadily, never changing, over all the years of her life.

Close to sleep now, she all at once sees Billie again, long-awaited and vividly beautiful. Billie enters the club, with her straining gray dog ahead of her: Billie holds the leash up high, she holds her head high, her lovely face, and after Billie and the dog comes the slouch-hatted man with his bandaged hand.

Of course that was how they entered, in that order.

4 / In Paris

In Paris, Daria and Smith go to dinner at Maxim's; a great treat, a celebration. The two of them, married one whole week. Married!

But is that possible, only one week since the minister began it all, "Dearly beloved—" in the orchard, in the familiar smells of apple and grass? Eliza looking sad, and Josephine scowling (why?), and little Catherine happy as a kitten. One week: is it possible that they are now at Maxim's, on an elegant French evening?

Everything there, at Maxim's, pleases Smith greatly; he is almost swollen with pleasure: their table, a good one; the waiters; and the smooth bare well-tended, well-braceleted arms of the women in the room, all in silk or chiffon, expensive fabrics; and the portentous but well-tanned men in black ties. The mirrors, returning all that, in their Art Nouveau frames. Smoke, perfume.

Smith whispers, "Do you know some of the richest people in the world are in this room tonight?"

"Really? Sounds like a good place for a bomb." Daria did not mean to say this; it "slips out," and then she giggles, and then coughs, and sips champagne. And tries to taste her dessert, a peach with ice cream. Pêche Melba.

Smith frowns, and then smiles too quickly, too reassuringly.

Daria closes her eyes against everything, and then for an instant she has a quick apocalyptic vision: Maxim's *is* bombed; blood and money and champagne and food pour out into the Rue Royale, diamonds and gold spouting out from windows like fireworks. And a crowd of poor people gathers to sift through the spoils, to wash off the jewels and cash. She opens her eyes; the opulent room is still there, quite safe. Of course it is.

They are staying—or, rather, they were staying at the Ritz. Now, because Daria kept getting lost there (silly, really, but there were so many corridors, so lined with such dazzling displays, such diamonds and gold, such crystal), now they are staying at a smaller, more comprehensible hotel, the Montalembert. Except that Daria is afraid of the elevator: a small slow glass cage, with bronze fittings. She does not tell Smith of this fear; he was so nice (sweet, really) about leaving the Ritz. In fact, she senses that he likes his indulgent-husband role: "Darling, you really don't like it here, do you? Well, easiest thing, we'll move." But she senses too that his indulgence will only go so far; she does not want to make him nervous, to be worrisome, an interference with his larger plans.

After the dinner at Maxim's the elevator makes her terribly dizzy; when they get to the room, she is sick in the bathroom. Too much rich food, Smith thinks smilingly.

Strangely, the bed at the Montalembert feels exactly like the bed at the Ritz: large and soft and terrifying. Hot, smelling of failure and of slime—odors available only to Daria; Smith doesn't notice.

And a new word has entered Daria's mind: Fuck. That is what they do, what Smith does to her, repeatedly. Before marrying they kissed a lot, he gently touched her breasts, and that was nice, and she had thought that "intercourse," the word she used before this new one, would be an extension of kissing, a loving transaction between two people, two people "in love." But not so: now she is being "fucked," and the word itself, its presence in her mind, makes her shudder with its ugliness, its dirt.

Obviously, Smith enjoys what he does, or he wouldn't do it so often, would he?

Sometimes Daria wishes for Eliza, so that she could ask her—but ask her what? Use what words? "Eliza, do you like to 'fuck'?" She has a feeling that Eliza does.

But Daria is perfectly happy in Paris, really, and the city is so perfectly beautiful—although that September there is a heat wave, yellowing, bleaching, almost paralyzing the city—so happy, so beautiful, that she cries a great deal of the time.

That perfect space, that vista from Notre Dame—the Tuileries Garden, then the Champs, wide and rising to the Arc—it is lovely enough to break your heart.

And the slow dark Seine, its gray stone embankments, gray stone bridges, fishermen, alone; of course she cries.

She and Smith are a perfect couple, too, beautiful and young and just-married Americans. A couple probably about to live happily ever after, with a lot of children and money and houses in the country.

They are sitting on the terrace of the Flore, pretty, thin Daria in her sleeveless yellow linen, yellow-eyed (she can see herself in everyone else's eyes), in the yellow September heat. And Smith, who is warm and flushed, very handsome today, is telling her about having come to Paris before, his boisterous undergraduate trip. The Tabu and the Méphisto, Bal Nègre. Juliette Greco. Pernod. "Well, I really didn't know what had hit me," Smith is boyishly saying. "I've always had a sort of weakness for licorice, and we really lapped it up that night, like it was going out of style."

He pauses to light his pipe, as Daria thinks how handsome, how perfect he is. But what has he been talking about?

". . . West Indian dancing," he says, and laughs. She must have lost her place.

She feels like crying. But everything is perfect, isn't it? "Smith?"

5 / Office Work

Eliza's income from the few stocks that Caleb Hamilton, her father, left amounted to about half of what she had estimated that, minimally, she and Catherine would need to live on; thus, she had had a series of part-time jobs. Economically a full-time job would have made more sense. She knew that; she was often broke, often worried. But working full-time left her much less time for Catherine—and no time at all for her own work, her secret poems.

Josephine, who was visibly very well off indeed, sometimes sent checks—always welcome, a help; but Josephine felt that Eliza should support herself, and Eliza agreed. At thirty, she should certainly not be dependent on Josephine.

Early on, Eliza was classified as a Medical Secretary, and so she remained, with one vaguely medical job after another. But it was strange, that series of medical settings; sometimes Eliza thought it another (probably futile) opposition to Josephine, for whom "scientific" was a nearly dirty word. "The scientific mind" was always uttered with Josephine's most Bostonian scorn. In any case, locked into her Medical Secretary label, Eliza rather liked it there—in a furtive way she liked doctors, was excited by medicine.

. . .

From shortly after Daria's wedding, that August, until late January, she worked in the research annex of a hospital, in a room labeled "Cardiac Data Retrieval."

Late January in San Francisco, which sometimes includes the week of Chinese New Year, can be and often is insane. Ferociously cold days of lashing rains are abruptly succeeded by sunny days of summer temperatures, when unnaturally bright grass grows suddenly in all the parks, as if overnight—when no one knows what to wear and everyone feels more than a little crazy, and crazy people feel much crazier than usual.

In Eliza's office, a small fierce girl, the head of that office, the "supervisor," stood beside the huge open window, violently inhaling the sultry outside air and cursing the world. Kathleen Mooney, twenty-six, with bright yellow-brown hair and a pale, wide, often open mouth, and a truly encyclopedic knowledge of the human heart: its functioning, possible anomalies and lesions, and the probable corrective operations. She also remembered everything about every patient whose files had passed through her office during the past two years of her employment. And all this with no medical training; she had an extraordinary "scientific mind," and Eliza had more than once thought how Josephine would dislike Kathleen—had even imagined their confrontation: Josephine's ice versus the rage of Kathleen.

Kathleen's general reaction to the universe, to being alive and to most other living beings, *was* rage, simple and pure and not concealed. And the untimely heat, of course, made her worse. "Drop dead of an aneurism, or a myocardial infarction," she audibly mouthed in the direction of the chief heart surgeon, Dr. Gilbert Branner, who was then crossing the street from the research building to the hospital. And then, turning back to the room, to her audience of two co-workers, "Lord!" she said. "He's always touching his hair. Lord, what an old peacock that man is."

Next to Kathleen's desk was Eliza's. The third desk, nearest the door, was Miriam's. Miriam, a tall very black girl with thin legs, a big stomach and big breasts. Eighteen years old, still living with her mother and her brothers in a nearby ghetto called "the Project." Her face was very black; she hated its color. Actually it had wonderful and complicated shades of brown; that was what Eliza thought of Miriam's face—not Miriam.

Eliza, though young herself, was the "older woman" of the group; also, since she only worked part-time, mornings, she was regarded as being of another, superior class. By Miriam she was regarded as rich: she owned a house; she went out with a lot of men, sometimes to expensive places.

Actually, Eliza at that time was in a curious phase that neither Kathleen nor Miriam knew about: she who indeed had gone out with a lot of men, who for a time went from one love affair to another, precipitously (she sometimes had an unpleasant vision of someone playing leapfrog), had not been going out at all. Having broken, finally, with her most recent lover, The Lawyer, her improbable choice for a brief fling at monogamy (she broke with him on the night she returned from Daria's wedding), she stayed at home with Catherine. She read a lot. She finished two new poems. But she did not need to discuss any of that at work; it was much easier to maintain her prescribed (by Kathleen) stereotype: sexy, impractical, bright but lazy. Rich.

Kathleen's sexual pattern, too, had just undergone a sudden change; for the first time she had "fallen in love." Before that she had had tidy arrangements with married men; encounters that were brief and emotionally unencumbered. "Well, let's face it, I like to screw" had been her explanation. "And I don't dig a lot of emotional mess." Eliza envied the practicality of that view, as she sometimes envied Kathleen's trim and tidy athletic body; her own voluptuousness seemed messy.

Kathleen fell in love with a boy of about her own age: Lawry, a sometime guitarist. And she, who often spoke harshly of her lovers, spoke only praise of Lawry. But Lawry, for whatever reasons (to Eliza they were very suspect), insisted that

Kathleen continue with her singles' bars and married men, and so she did. "Christ, sometimes I feel like some kind of an exhibition fucker," said Kathleen.

All three of those women smoked too much, especially Kathleen, who exhaled with furious gusts.

In the heat, that day, they were all wearing summer dresses. Kathleen's was a floral print, too bright, overwhelming her light coloring—but she had made it herself; she liked that dress. Miriam wore a black linen sheath, loose-fitting, which she hoped concealed her breasts. Eliza's dress was a faded blue chambray from some past and plumper time of her life; it rather hung about her, giving her a look that was both lost and provocative.

All day, every day, Kathleen talked, almost nonstop. Now, with no transition from her cursing of Dr. Branner, she began to talk about Lawry, who had recently moved down to Los Angeles. "His card said 'See you soon,'" she said. "*Soon* could very well mean this weekend, couldn't it? I'd better bake some bread, and I'll get some beef and make a stew. Lawry really loves my bread, and that good stew."

Miriam and Eliza did not exchange looks, but each felt the other's reaction; it was sadly clear to both of them that Lawry did not love Kathleen, that he had probably moved down to Los Angeles to get away from her. Their feelings, Eliza's and Miriam's, were often similar; for Kathleen they both felt a combination of affection and annoyance—she talked so much— and fear; Eliza and Miriam were both women who would do a great deal to avoid anger, a scene.

"Tomorrow night I'll bake some bread and wash my hair," said Kathleen.

"You want the things from the cath lab now?" asked Miriam, stretching and yawning.

"What? Oh, sure, you might as well." Kathleen sighed, feeling interrupted. And then, as Miriam ambled out, she muttered to Eliza, "Honestly, she's half asleep. I don't know what she does at night."

"Insomnia, maybe." Eliza was made nervous by Kathleen's reactions to Miriam. Kathleen was an army brat, her father a master sergeant who lived in Fort Bragg, North Carolina; supposedly, statedly, she was in rebellion against army attitudes, and Southern ones, but about Miriam she could be small-minded, mean.

"More likely chasing around the joints on Fillmore Street," snorted Kathleen. "Honestly, the belle of the Amazon."

Eliza had understood for some time that Kathleen was jealous of Miriam, jealous of the fact that many men were after Miriam, phoning her, following her on the street. Eliza even pointed this out to Miriam, trying to explain some of Kathleen's anger. But Miriam could not accept that theory: a white girl, with an apartment, and a car, too—jealous of *her?* Somebody's got to be kidding.

"Oh, it's so hot," said Eliza then, and she went over to the window to stand with Kathleen and observe the street, and the hospital across the way.

Dr. Branner was standing on the steps talking to someone in a lab coat—an intern, or a research fellow. It was true that he was vain, Eliza thought, but who would not be? A man looking like that, at his age (fifty—fifty-five?). He was tall and thin, with thick white hair, a year-round tan (he sailed) and startling light green eyes. Sea eyes, Eliza thought, from some remote northern sea. He was married, very rich and said to be promiscuous. A few of his affairs were notorious, had involved "socially prominent" and beautiful young women.

"I wonder who he's crawling into bed with now," mused Kathleen. "I'm sure he's too much of a snob for nurses."

"I wouldn't"—Eliza began, and then she changed the end of her sentence—"have any idea," she finished, having realized with horror that she had been about to say: I wouldn't mind.

. . .

An important fact about that office was that almost nothing was actually done in it. The walls were covered with books containing loose-leafed data on patients who had had some form of heart surgery. And at intervals patients came back for checkups, and more data was added to the files. Or they died: an additional fact. Sometimes a doctor or a research fellow would come to the door, first cautiously knocking (everyone was a little afraid of Kathleen), and say that he was working on a paper, and wanted a specific piece of information. How many ASDs among female patients over forty? Kathleen always understood the question—Eliza often did not, nor did Miriam. And a couple of days later Kathleen would send the list, by Miriam, and often the researcher phoned to express gratitude.

But the list only took Kathleen half an hour to pull together. Eliza, who contrary to Kathleen's view was neither lazy nor inefficient (nor was Miriam), had calculated that instead of two and a half people in that office, so to speak, one half-time person could easily do all the work. But Kathleen and Miriam seriously needed their full-time jobs, and Eliza needed her job.

Eliza had made that same calculation in other offices, at other jobs. What they all needed, of course, was "meaningful work," and an income. But her own meaningful work, her poetry, provided no income at all, and it was hard to imagine much better solutions for Kathleen or for Miriam.

She even, sometimes, in moments of paralyzing boredom, imagined complaining that they had not enough to do, but to whom would she complain? Dr. Branner? This, of course, was unthinkable. Her relationship with him was almost nonexistent, but still curious; he addressed Kathleen, the supervisor of that room, as "Kathleen," whereas he sometimes addressed Eliza, the part-time underling, the Medical Secretary, with a murmured "Mrs. Quarles." He was never known to show any awareness of Miriam, the File Clerk.

Kathleen was highly aware of his distinctions. "Social class, that's all he cares about. He digs your Eastern accent, *Mrs.* Quarles. The fucking old snob."

. . .

On Fridays, wearing lab coats and carrying efficient-looking clipboards, on which nothing was ever written, Kathleen and Eliza crossed the street to the hospital; down a maze of halls—sometimes passing white-sheeted patients on gurneys, waiting for something—they came at last to the rear entrance of the amphitheatre. There they found seats, from which to observe what was called the Surgical Conference, a presentation and discussion of patients who were possible candidates for surgery.

The front seats were traditionally taken by the surgeons, on the right, and on the left were the cardiologists. Behind them sat interns, fellows and med students.

The surgeons arrived as a group, behind Dr. Branner, who, with his swinging, leisurely, but athletic saunter, always led the rest. They were often spoken of as a team, and Eliza saw that they had indeed that look; they could have been heading for a football bench. And the others seemed to imitate Gilbert Branner's walk; like him, they all sauntered, with a swing to their gaits. The cardiologists came in separately, or in groups of two or three, and as a group they were less easily defined, except that most of them were Jewish. None of the surgeons was Jewish; to Eliza, a very suspicious fact.

An intern came up to the lectern, and in a soft Southern voice he began to speak. He reminded Eliza of Evan; lately she had been thinking too much of her dead husband—a part of her unnaturally celibate condition, she had decided. The intern described a white female of fifty-seven, a heavy smoker. Dypsnea on exertion, some angina. A history of rheumatic fever.

Eliza's attention to what was being said had gone, and she began to watch gestures instead. Gilbert Branner (Gilbert?) was inattentively stretching his long legs; he already knew that they should operate, and that a woman of fifty-seven had a "pretty fair chance," as he liked to put it. Dr. Stern, the chief cardiologist, was avidly listening, storing up information to be used in argument; he would want to continue with a course of medication, and to postpone surgery for as long as possible.

"A young woman, slightly overweight, occasional attacks of anxiety, some insomnia, a smoker, sexually somewhat promiscuous—" They were talking about her, Eliza; she was vividly hallucinating the presentation of herself. And they continued; they decided that something must be done about her heart. In the ensuing debate, Dr. Branner won out over Dr. Stern. Gilbert was going to cut into and open up her heart. (Gilbert!)

Of course they were not talking about Eliza. They were looking at some X-rays, illuminated on a large screen next to the lectern. "Some calcification, possible shunting, a clear mitral."

Dizzily, Eliza decided to attend fully to the next case, a two-year-old boy with Down's Syndrome—which, on the way out, Kathleen explained fully to her: a Mongoloid, he will die anyway; they won't operate.

Eliza more or less took in what Kathleen said, but she still felt agitated, uncertain and upset. In the increasing, powerful heat, as the day moved toward noon, she and Kathleen slowly crossed the street to the research building, where their office was. A block farther on there was an open grassy park, raised up from the street, where a dark young man, bearded and in shirt sleeves, was sitting at ease in the sun. Eliza imagined running down to him and saying—saying what? Inviting?

Dr. Branner and his retinue of surgeons hurried past the two young women. Passing, their white lab coats were stiff and resistant to the heat. Dr. Branner's fine white hair was all in place—all beautiful.

Just then Eliza came to an understanding with herself. She recognized that she did not want an "affair" with Gilbert Branner, an exploitive married man; she had been through that already with The Consul. She wanted to go to bed with Branner once, and not again. A one-night or one-afternoon stand. She smiled, thinking that such an impulse was supposed to be a man's prerogative. And she considered a further, corollary fact about men: they do not like to be dropped after one encounter; they like it even less than women do. Once Eliza had done this—to, of all people, an Iranian banker, partly under a misapprehension that he was leaving the next day for Switzerland, for good. The next day he telephoned, not going to Switzerland, after all, and was furious at her refusal to see him again. (This helped to confirm his view that all American women were whores, and the following year he married a distant cousin, a decent Persian girl.)

"Why are you smiling?" Kathleen asked. They had entered the research building and started down the hall.

"No real reason." And then Eliza asked, "Kathleen, have you ever thought about going to med school?" As she asked this, it struck her as incredible that she had not asked before—of course, that was what Kathleen should do.

Striding ahead of Eliza, Kathleen had just opened the door. Miriam raised her head from her arms, which were crossed on the desk. To Eliza, Miriam looked as though she had something to say, but Kathleen had begun to shout.

"Have I ever thought about going to med school? Lord, don't you know the first thing? How much it costs and how hard it is to get in, especially for women? And I'd have to go back to college and get more science credits. Can't you just see me in the chem lab at William and Mary, with all those darling coeds in cashmere and pearls and loafers? Eliza, you don't *think*."

Miriam was indeed trying to say something, but Kathleen was still focused on Eliza. "Besides," she went on, "I don't want to be a doctor. I don't even want to work. I want to be a wife, like everyone else, and have some kids. Just because you've already got a kid, Eliza—"

Miriam got out, "Lawry—"

Those syllables reached Kathleen. She turned on Miriam and shouted, "*What?*"

Slowly, Miriam smiled (beautifully); she said, "He call."

"You black bitch!" But that was affectionate; Kathleen could only have said it in a mood of great warmth toward Miriam. "What did he say?"

"He say he at some place—The Lion's Share?"

"Lord, that's in San Anselmo. He played there for a while. Oh, Lord, he could be here in an hour."

"No, he say he got business to tend to there. He be on along this afternoon."

For an instant Kathleen's radiant face was dimmed, but then, "That's better, really," she said. She laughed softly. "If I know him, which I certainly do, I'll have plenty of time for everything." And in an excited but at the same time methodical way, she began to organize her desk. She picked up her bag, got up and headed for the door; then she turned, and her voice had reverted to its old anger as she said, "Now don't you girls think you can leave just because I'm gone. And if anyone calls or comes in, you figure out something to say, you hear?"

They both nodded.

"And, Miriam, when Eliza goes don't you spend the afternoon asleep or talking on the phone. Don't you dare!"

She opened the door, then smiled in a tentative small way, and in quite another voice she said, "And wish me luck."

Left alone, Eliza and Miriam smiled weakly at each other—both burdened with the warring emotions that Kathleen always produced. Miriam said, "Let's us pray," and they both laughed a little.

When Miriam and Eliza had first met, the previous fall, Eliza had made a few efforts to talk seriously to her, or at least to mention some of the things that were happening to black people at that time. She spoke about the Freedom Riders, Dr. King. But she soon understood that while Miriam thought it was wrong for people not to get to go where they wanted, she did not understand the fuss about registering voters; she could barely be persuaded that people should vote—she never had. Her ambition was to be a Secretary, not a File Clerk. She had never heard of Billie Holiday. She was crazy about Elvis Presley.

Finally, Eliza understood that Miriam liked her for being "rich" and well-dressed, the owner of a house. Which was not exactly how Eliza saw herself, but those were things that Miriam hungrily aspired to, that were even beyond her aspirations.

Then one afternoon, in her usual soft conversational voice, Miriam told Eliza this brief story: a couple of years ago (she would have been sixteen) she had this boyfriend, Thomas, and they got along real good, she really liked Thomas. And she and Thomas had this friend, a white fellow who lived on Pine Street, near the Project. Jasper. They used to fool around together, smoke some grass, drink beer. And one time they were fooling around with this gun that Jasper had. And Jasper put it up to Thomas's head and it went off. Thomas fell down and brains and blood spilled out. It looked so—*terrible*.

They had an inquest. Jasper was acquitted. An accident.

Miriam thought it was an accident too; she couldn't really blame Jasper. Still, she had wondered how it would have been if it had been Thomas with the gun, blowing off the head of Jasper, a white person.

(Eliza wondered too.)

What was most devastating to Eliza was Miriam's acceptance; this was the sort of thing that could happen, any time. At any moment the friend you love could get blown up right in front of you.

Miriam even seemed anxious not to make too much of it. "I felt real bad for a long time after that," she said. "I don't know—"

"*Christ*, Miriam, of course you did."

Miriam never referred to this story again, nor to Thomas, and neither, of course, did Eliza.

And so, when left alone, when not complaining or sighing over Kathleen, Eliza and Miriam generally talked about clothes.

"I was to the Emporium last night," said Miriam, "and there was these make-believe fur coats?" Miriam's observations often came in the form of questions, as though she doubted the evidence of her senses. "Oooh, they was pretty, I'm telling you. *Real* pretty."

"Miriam, you'd be paying for one of those coats for a year. And long after you got tired of it. You buy too much stuff." Of course this was true, Eliza had said it before, and it would never take effect. "Why don't you make a list of what you need for a year?" she asked once more, wearily.

"You right, I reckon I should."

Outside, in the high noon heat, the slightest breeze had arisen, barely enough to rattle the stiff yellow leaves that had fallen in the gutters. On the other side of San Francisco, along Grant Avenue, preparations were being made for the Chinese New Year. That night there would be a parade, and the sounds of Chinese flutes and mandolins, firecrackers and human shouts would all be audible as far away as Russian Hill, where Eliza's cottage was. Where, some blocks away, Dr. Branner occupied the penthouse of an expensive new apartment building.

"I'd really like to go on home," Eliza said. "You don't think Kathleen will call?"

"Naw, you go on. She call, I tell her something."

Eliza grinned. "You're great. Well, have a good weekend. Happy Chinese New Year."

"Yeah. You, too."

Eliza started down the hall. As she turned the corner toward the bank of elevators, Dr. Branner—Gilbert Branner—was emerging from his office, as she almost knew he would be. He had bent down to lock his door.

Eliza said, "Oh, hi!" And she achieved with her voice and her stance a remarkable transformation: as he straightened to look at her, he saw suddenly that she was not an office worker (and no one would be more aware of that than Gilbert Branner) but an attractive young blond woman, of a certain education (Eastern), a certain social style.

"Hi, how are you?" he asked, smiling at her, and achieving

at least for himself a vigorous sound of youth. "Hot enough for you?"

"Unbelievable!"

The elevator was there, and together they entered and descended, smiling at each other in a companionable and pleased way. Eliza said, "You wouldn't be driving over to Russian Hill now, would you?"

"Well, yes, is that where you live, too? I didn't know— what luck!"

"Yes, marvelous," she agreed.

They walked out toward his open car, with their separate but momentarily coincident plans, into the unnatural, sweltering afternoon.

6 / *Phone Calls and Firecrackers*

By the following Sunday the heat had not abated, nor had the Chinese New Year celebrations appreciably calmed down; to Eliza, alone in her Russian Hill cottage, both the weather and the festive sounds seemed exotic and unreal. And she herself had a curious feeling of suspension, of aimless waiting and undefined need.

Catherine had gone across town for lunch and a movie with her best friend, and Eliza had a free day, with which, uncharacteristically, she could not decide what to do. And it was as though her vague needs were transmitted into the air as messages—and received by various friends, who telephoned.

First Kathleen, in her staccato, nonstop way: "That fucking Lawry, do you know he never showed up on Friday? He calls me in the middle of the night, really stoned. All I needed. Doesn't want to come up or anything, and God forbid we should screw; he just wants to talk. I hung up on him, and then I went out to a bar, you know, the old body-shop routine, but I really couldn't take it. It made me sick, and so I went on home. Jesus, men. I may give the whole thing up and get a dildo. Well, how are you? What's that crazy noise at your house?"

"Firecrackers. Chinese New Year."

"Oh, really? And then he called me this morning, like we were friends, asking when he gets to meet my secretary. Not you, Mrs. Quarles, *Miriam.* That rotten bastard got a look at her one time—he'd come by the office to see me and she was strutting across the street, high, probably—and ever since he's been pestering me, teasing me about her. Shit, I think I will introduce them, they deserve each other. Well, see you tomorrow."

Hanging up, Eliza recognized that the conversation had made her extremely uneasy. Although Kathleen's anger was never directed at her, still Eliza felt and was vaguely frightened by its force; its hostile weight battered against her. And she truly hated Kathleen's rage at Miriam. Sometimes Eliza felt so protective of Miriam that she had considered adopting her, and then had thought, Do I really need an eighteen-year-old black daughter?

To combat her unease, she created some minor chores for herself.

She went into the kitchen, where she got out the blender and a bowl of leftover vegetables for soup, a thrifty habit she had learned early from Josephine—to whom frugality was a virtue, if *haute cuisine* was not.

What Eliza really wanted to be doing was any one of three other things: waxing a newly stripped walnut coffee table, walking in the marvelous light air outside or working on a poem. But perhaps she did not want to do any of those strongly enough? she was truly suspended between wants? As she saw it just then, those were treats to be saved for later on. In the meantime, having ground the vegetables and added chicken soup, she cleaned the blender and turned her attention to the inside of the stove.

She decided that when the phone rang next she would not answer it, knowing quite well what was coming: an inevitable and unpleasant call from Gilbert Branner, of whom she had managed not to think.

The previous Friday afternoon had been entirely terrible for him: a humiliation. For her it was sad and embarrassing. And unpleasant: unable to perform, he had commanded help from her, and she complied, despite distaste (and was that why her help hadn't worked?), despite annoyance at her own compliant, female nature. She ended more annoyed at herself than at him. And afterward she even thought that she would have to see him again, when he asked, as he surely would, just for the sake of his aging and vulnerable ego. But then she thought, No, I've done too much of that, too much yielding and pretending, and it's too expensive for me. Why should I see him again, when I don't want to at all, and when he can easily find someone who likes and values him more than I do?

She went upstairs with a vague plan about going through old winter clothes, then reminded herself that winter was only in abeyance, that the insane heat was not a sign of spring. Yet it was with a sort of springtime dreaming lethargy that she fell across her bed, looking out the window at the small garden below in which some of the shrubbery had been deceived into a sudden flowering.

By the time the phone rang, she had forgotten not to answer it.

Gilbert Branner said, "Well, what luck to find you at home on such an exceptionally beautiful Sunday."

She murmured something, and trusted that her sound was polite.

"I was hoping I could persuade you to come out for a little while on my boat. It's a perfect day for the Bay."

Not if it has berths, it occurred to Eliza to say. Instead she said, "That's terribly nice, but I promised my daughter a walk through Chinatown. New Year's is still going on."

At that he chuckled. "Say, do you want to hear a good one?" And he told her a joke about Chinese girls that was racist, sexist, unfunny but mercifully short.

"Well," he said, and he had begun to sound a little awkward; were her unsaid thoughts traversing the few blocks' distance between them? He attempted a little laugh. "I do think we should have a rerun sometime. A new start?"

She murmured something negative, aware of rising tension—a tightening in her throat.

He said, "Of course it's entirely up to you, but I do think you're being a little unjust, if I may say so." His tone had hardened and grown colder as he spoke, so that the last phrase was pure ice.

"It's not just that—" It's not your sexual performance, or lack of it; it's everything about you, she would have liked to say. I thought you'd be fun for an afternoon. My mistake, not yours. But I really don't like you at all, any more than—probably—you like most of the girls you screw.

None of which she was able to say to Gilbert Branner. Instead she said, "I'm really sorry."

"You know, I ordinarily don't spend much time with secretaries." Was that his notion of the *coup de grâce?*

"So I understand." Eliza was unable not to say this.

An iced pause. And then the real *coup de grâce:* "Well, you actually won't fall into that category much longer. The grant that supports your job runs out next month. The other two— uh—ladies will stay on, of course."

Was that true? Could she now be free of jobs, collecting unemployment money? As she hung up, Eliza was breathless with the possibility.

And having said that she was going to walk through Chinatown, that was what she did, in the heat, in the bedraggled remnants of the New Year celebration.

She walked down Vallejo Street to Columbus, and then right, toward Broadway; hurried across to Grant Avenue, to Chinatown. There the old ladies, clutching tattered shopping bags, walked sideways on their ruined feet past the cheap bright Western-style stores and the Chinese markets that displayed exotic vegetables and fish and barbecued chickens and duck. Thin dark young Oriental men, dressed in black business suits for the holiday, sauntered along the street, and almond-eyed children darted in and out of alleys, while firecrackers spurted like machine guns. The gutters were littered with sodden bright confetti.

Back in her own house, an hour or so later, Eliza was tired, but some of the day's earlier trouble had drained or evaporated from her mind. With a cup of tea she sat comfortably at her kitchen table, savoring the rare luxury of no thoughts at all.

And then the phone rang. And because it could be Catherine saying something about when she was coming home—saying anything—for the third time that day Eliza answered the ring.

It was a friend from college, Peggy Kennerlie, inviting her to a party in Belvedere, some weeks off. Eliza accepted, out of habit, and then wondered why: she was tired of both the Kennerlies; she had been tired of Kennerlie parties for years. Maybe she wouldn't go.

She began to see this series of calls as some form of punishment—or possibly a test?

Another call. An unmistakable soft voice said, "Hey, Eliza, this is Miriam. How're you doing?"

"Oh, I'm fine. Are you okay?"

"Yeah, real okay." She laughed, her rich rounded laughter that meant affection for Eliza, and that also signaled that she was high, on God knows what. "Say, Eliza, do you know the last name of Lawry? Kathleen's Lawry?"

"Lawry? No, I don't."

"Well, it's got to be the one. He call me, say he seen me, say could I meet him for a drink."

"Christ, Miriam. Kathleen would kill you."

"You right, and anyway I'm not about to meet him for a drink. I don't drink!" And she laughed again, prolonged, and *high*.

. . .

Eliza's last phone call was from Daria, calling from New York, to say that she was pregnant. "Two months, a baby next August—it could come on your birthday! Eliza, isn't that fantastic! I can't believe it. I've always wanted—we'd like a dozen children, Smith and I. Eliza, isn't it *great?*"

7 / Miriam

Tall and beautiful, stoop-shouldered, Miriam shuffled across the hard bare neglected yard of the Project, in the morning, on her way to work. She was wearing tight new black shoes and a big brown coat. Even though the coat hid most of her body, she still stooped—she always had; and she walked with her head lowered, through the bunches of skinny little kids on their way to school, with their books and funny little bags of lunch.

She was hungry; quarreling at breakfast with her mother, her stomach had closed up and she couldn't eat. Her mother was light-skinned and had dyed her hair blond, and she was mean. Her mother said Miriam was mean: "The blacker the meaner. You just like your father, just exactly. Sulking. Black and mean." Maybe she was mean, but just because she got a raise at work was she supposed to make payments on her mother's living-room sofa from the Emporium? Even if some of the stains were from Cokes and things that she and her friends had spilled when they got high?

She wanted a Coke now, but she was late, and it was faster to walk than take a bus to the hospital, the office. Where Kathleen might or might not be mad.

Quarreling with her mother, in those small crowded rooms, with her brothers and sisters watching, filled Miriam with need. She needed to scream and hit and cry, and she wildly wanted everything in the world that was not her mother, not the Project. She wanted more shoes and outfits, and velvet sofas and tall gold lamps with pleated shades, and big white refrigerators full of food, and fast white cars—things like you could win in a contest. Like the Christmas windows at Macy's or Sears. All that wanting sometimes made her sick.

Along Fillmore Street, where she walked, among the small greasy restaurants that had barbecue and hamburgers and Mexican food, there were a lot of new little stores that sold funny things: old dresses with yellow lace on them, and old-timey men's suits with big shoulders and big white buttons. Who'd want that stuff? But some of the stores sold real nice things, some nice new outfits, in these bad colors. But it all cost money.

She stopped to look at some purple velvet pants with a tunic top, wondering, Would I look good in that? Look long and thin? There was always layaway. In front of the outfit, reflected in the glass, she saw her own face, big and black, with kinky hair that she hadn't had time to iron out that morning.

Then, making her jump and turn around quickly, a man's voice said, "You're a girl that likes nice things."

She turned toward him, and he had to be a pimp, in those sharp tight clothes: wine suede bell-bottoms and a black silk turtleneck stretched tight across his chest. But he looked nice, too; he looked good.

"Some, not too much," she said, and she lifted her head and started to walk on up the street.

Being tall, he kept up with her—no trouble for him. "You look good," he said. "I really dig the way you look."

"Lucky you." She walked faster, because it had crazily come to her that what she wanted to say was: Okay, then, why don't you pay me for looking good? You think it happens free?

"You work?" he asked.

"Yeah." Her sigh said what she thought of her job: the details that made no sense and that turned into mistakes, the boredom, Kathleen, who was always talking and mad, and her low, low pay.

"Maybe you in the wrong line." He laughed.

A pimp. They all came on the same. She knew. She said, "Maybe *you* in the wrong line of work."

He laughed again. "You think you know? You ever think to be a model? Get money just to wear nice clothes?"

Knowing better, still her heart raced. Had she ever thought? Just all the time. Herself in long white fur coats, with shoes that matched, and cameras all turned on her. Ten, fifteen dollars an hour. *Could* he be not a pimp? "I'm late for work," she said.

"You come back this way? When you get off? I'll be looking for you after five. I might have a little Valentine for you." He touched her arm, so that she stopped, and she looked at him again. He was blacker than she was, with eyes that slanted up, and a sharp little beard on his chin. "Well, so long," he said, and he made a sort of salute to her with a casual, loosely clasped-up fist. "I'll see you, baby," and he laughed.

She scowled, not knowing what to make of him, what to do, and she turned away with her chin up. Let him find her again if he could.

"Miriam, you're late!" Kathleen screamed out, in the office.

But Miriam, who listened for tone more than words, knew that Kathleen was mad because she had something to tell.

Miriam changed into a lab coat, which hid her almost as well, and she said, "You hear from Lawry?"

Not at all intuitive herself, Kathleen was always amazed by Miriam. "You Geminis," she said. "I think maybe he's coming up this weekend. I got another see-you-soon card."

"I reckon he could be coming."

"God, the crumbs I live on! And after that last no-show trip. I *know* I should dump him."

Kathleen had this idea that she, Miriam, understood everything she said, but Miriam did not; nothing about Kathleen made any sense to Miriam. There she was, white and over twenty, been to college, making good money being a supervisor, but she never bought any clothes, just paid rent and spent money on her little car, and all hung up on this guy who had no money and moved to Los Angeles and only came up every four or five weeks to see her, and then half the time didn't show.

Even Eliza made more sense to Miriam than Kathleen did; she missed Eliza, and didn't understand about her getting fired. "I made him fire me so I could get unemployment," Eliza had explained, seeming happy about the whole thing. Kathleen did not miss Eliza, and said mean things about her all the time.

"Tonight I'll have to wash my hair and bake bread, in case he comes," Kathleen said, as she so often had before. "God, why can't I just tell him to shove it, will you tell me that?"

"You like him." She did not say—of course not—that Lawry called her; not postcards—phone calls, from Los Angeles. Said he had to meet her. But she refused.

"Oh, I guess."

It was hard for Miriam to listen to Kathleen all day. Miriam felt that her own life was terrible, but at least it was familiar to her; she knew all her own troubles even if she couldn't lift them off. But Kathleen's pinched and furious world was strange. And so sometimes Miriam talked just to make Kathleen be quiet.

"There was this guy talking to me on the way to work," she said. "And he looked real good, in these bad pants, but I don't know if he be a pimp. He had on these far-out clothes?"

This was of course not a question, but Kathleen chose to answer. "Miriam, you stay away from people like that! Like that guy who said he was going to take you to Vegas. Don't you read the papers? Girls beaten up, stabbed to death?"

"I know, but he *might* not be one. He did look good. There anything you'd like for me to do?"

Kathleen sighed. She would rather have gone on talking,

but she was conscientious, in her way—or, rather, terrified of being caught lacking. And so she said, "You can go to the cath lab and see if the caths on Gonzales and Hardy are ready. And have them copied. You know."

Miriam walked out of the research building and across the street, to the hospital. Some people didn't like her and they frowned whenever they saw her. Mr. Graham, who was head of something in the business office. Or several of them didn't know what to do and so they pretended she wasn't there. Several of the doctors did that: Dr. Branner, Dr. Stern. But there were a couple of interns who were pretty nice, and they liked her and kidded around with her. "Hey, Miriam, you look like you're high!"

"Oh, I wish I was!"

What would it be like to have a white boyfriend? She had wondered about that sometimes. She thought that she would like to. But you didn't see near as many white boys with black girls as black men with whites. One of her brothers had a girl friend who was Spanish.

Kathleen hated everyone in the hospital, and sometimes Miriam thought she had been hired by Kathleen to make them all mad. The only other black people who worked there were orderlies or maids, and they looked at Miriam funny as she walked past in her white lab coat, with her black, black hair.

She got the typed cath reports and crossed the street back to the copying room, where a girl from the business office was using the machine, so Miriam had to wait. The girl had on this little short skirt and a bright yellow sweater; she was dressed in a hip way but you could tell she wasn't. Miriam did not know how. She was friendly—Lord, so friendly Miriam wanted to run.

"Miriam, how are you? I really love those shoes. You really look good in them but I just don't. I don't know what I'm going to do with all my skirts. You only got those three things to do? I can wait while you do them."

"No, you go on ahead."

Miriam sat down in a chair and closed her eyes, and she almost went to sleep, and she thought about these girls she knew who were whores, who lived in a big apartment on Twin Peaks; they'd had an interior decorator and had white carpets and white velvet sofas and gold lamps, and they wore all these different kinds of fur coats, and white shoes. She shuddered, thinking about it: what all did they have to *do?*

The friendly girl said, "Well, bye. Have a nice day."

As soon as Miriam got back to the office, Kathleen started up talking again. "And I've just realized there's a full moon in Scorpio this weekend! Anything could happen! He has three things in Scorpio, that's really heavy. I'll bet he does come up. I wonder how much dope I've got left. Why do I always have to provide everything, will you tell me that?"

"I don't know."

"I must really dig punishment. I guess I got it living all those years with my mother. Beating me up all the time. But if he doesn't like me why did he pick me up at the bar and come on like that? No one's ever come on at me in my life, not that way."

Miriam wondered about that, too. She wondered why anyone would pick Kathleen. Kathleen was so unlike being a woman at all; she was more like some skinny little boy who got in fights all the time. Lawry was good-looking in his pictures, with lots of straight light hair and those big pale eyes, but maybe a little girlish-looking. There had to be something funny about him somewhere, choosing Kathleen. He sure acted funny, from the sound of it.

Kathleen asked, "You want to come over to my house? I'll make some tuna sandwiches."

"Okay. I'll get us some Cokes."

They walked along Fillmore Street, in the opposite direction from where that man would be waiting for Miriam at five, or maybe he wouldn't be there—the man whom she would or would not go to meet.

Kathleen's place didn't have anything nice in it, just old furniture and Indian-looking things, but at least it was her own place. Miriam thought about getting herself a place, but she didn't want to until she could fix it up nice. At Kathleen's there was steam heat; it was always too hot there. In the Project nothing worked, and cold wind leaked in through the windows.

Sometimes Miriam wondered: Would she rather be her or Kathleen? Be Kathleen or be a hustler on Twin Peaks? Sometimes all the thinking that she did made her dizzy.

Kathleen brought in sandwiches and their Cokes, straws in the bottles, and they both sat on the wide day bed, which was the only place to sit.

Kathleen said, "If he could just settle down and we could have some kids. He really digs kids, we both do, and we could have one that was really beautiful. We wouldn't have to get married or anything like that."

"Be nice if he was at least *around*."

"That's true, you're absolutely right." Kathleen lit a cigarette and began to blow out smoke. Then she said, "You know, I've been thinking that Eliza was really more of a Leo than we always said. That grandstand way she left. I think basically she was a real Leo snob, and she couldn't stand it that Dr. Branner wouldn't pay any attention to her. She probably expected him to ask her out!"

Back at the office, there was really nothing to do. Kathleen stood at the window, staring out, smoking and cursing at random. "Damn you, Dr. Branner, I hope you break your neck. You, too, Dr. Stern."

Miriam in her mind could still see the man from this morning, see his slant devil eyes, and his black face, and it came to her that he could be anything at all: a photographer, looking for models; a plainclothes pig; a narc. A crazy junkie with a knife. Or a pimp. Or just a man, like her brothers.

He looked mostly like a pimp, but would that be, like, his disguise?

One time, she had heard about the funeral of a pimp, and

she had to laugh, it was so funny. Jimmy, the pimp, used to have this green Caddy with pale brown leather inside, and at the funeral there were all his whores, three black and two blond white girls, all wearing these green outfits, with pale brown leather trim. Still, Jimmy was dead, shot dead by the brother of a girl he'd pulled, one of his whores.

What did those guys have to say to pull a girl, to get her to be their whore?

Kathleen said, "Miriam! wake up. Suppose somebody comes in?"

Miriam could get home to the Project by walking along Webster Street and then down Steiner, instead of going along Fillmore, where he might be. But at five o'clock she still didn't know; she didn't know where to go.

"There was this bad purple outfit in the window this morning," she said to Kathleen, and she suddenly wished that Kathleen were Eliza, who would at least say something nice. But she went on anyway. "Tunic and pants—it was *bad*. Where I saw that guy."

"Lord, Miriam, all you think about is outfits. And guys." Together they turned off the lights, and locked up, and walked down the stairs to the street, where for a moment they stood in parting conversation.

Miriam laughed; suddenly she felt very good. "Sometimes you sound like my mother," she said. "Telling me what I don't need."

"You go to hell. Well, see you tomorrow. And you be on time!"

"Yeah, tomorrow."

And Miriam walked off toward Fillmore Street, to where she now knew he would be waiting for her, with something—a Valentine?—he would have something for her. An outfit? A ride in his car and some kind of offer of a job?

Some stuff for a great new high?

8 | A Sudden Marriage

"How about it?" asked the man—Larry? Harry?—in the pink-and-black jacket who was introduced to Eliza about ten minutes ago. "How about it? I've got the tickets in my pocket. We could take the red-eye flight to Acapulco, have breakfast and grab a car and on to . . ." The name of the Mexican town he mentioned was unintelligible, lost in the din of the Kennerlies' party. "We could be back by Wednesday or so," he added.

Laughing politely (she was like that, generally), Eliza excused herself with the truth. "I have to go to unemployment on Tuesday."

From Hollywood, although born in Berlin, Harry (not Larry) was used to people who did that; everyone sooner or later got unemployment checks. "Okay, sure," he answered easily. "Tuesday it is."

He did not, could not, know about her Tuesday traumas: the bus trips to a frightening part of town, Third and Bryant, standing in line with discouraged, tired people. Being given cash—being terrified.

In fact his reasonable tone, delivered in a still slightly Berlin-flavored accent, had begun to make Eliza wonder how could a reasonable man make such an insane suggestion. A very old-fashioned phrase even came to her mind: What kind of a girl do you think I am? And at the same time her imagination, which was quick and vivid, saw a stretching hot white Mexican beach, a tropical background of palms and manzanitas. Where they were, in Belvedere, across the Bay from San Francisco, it was a terribly cold dark day.

He even looked a little crazy, Harry did. His hair was a little too long for that time, its waves a little theatrical. His slightly protuberant blue eyes were too intense. (Too intense as she thought this, Eliza inwardly smiled; it was an odd phrase for one who had pursued intensity with lemming-like directness, who had generally thought the non-intense people were the crazy ones: Smith, her brother-in-law, and The Lawyer, her recent lover.) But the point was that, introduced to her fifteen minutes ago by their mutual host, Ted Kennerlie, this man was now asking her to go fly to Mexico for the weekend with him, in the midst of a perfectly ordinary California conversation about the length of the rainy season.

"The surf is really nice there, and the beach—" And just then, in mid-sentence, he surprised her again; he said, "Oh, my God, there's someone over there I've got to talk to. But I'll be back," and with a quick intense pale look he was gone, pushing through the crowded room toward the huge window, the mammoth view of San Francisco Bay. And Eliza was left to assume, naturally enough, that he had seen a prettier, more chic or more pliant-looking girl.

Not that she was especially insecure in matters of attractiveness; she knew that some men were strongly drawn to her, certainly not all, but who on earth would want all men? And as for chic, she knew, or wryly recognized, that at the Kennerlies' she tended to dress in conformity to their view of her, which is to say, to dress less well than she could. Now, in her black silk shirt, black skirt, she was aware that she looked vaguely arty, unsmart and somewhat waifish—exactly the Kennerlie and Kennerlie-friend view of her. They would not be at all surprised to hear that she now collected unemployment; they would view it as an eccentric joke, having themselves never been to Third and Bryant.

A remarkably homogeneous group, the other guests: attractive people in their late twenties, early thirties, who would all make a great deal of money in advertising, commercial art, architecture, something like that with a couple of bright young psychiatrists thrown in. The wives didn't do those things; they were busy having children, decorating "homes"—keeping the whole show going, as some of them liked to put it. (Peggy Kennerlie, the hostess and Eliza's college friend, often said this of herself.) And periodically Eliza came to these parties that the Kennerlies gave, and she wondered why. From one party to another she confused the names and faces—as they did hers: she is Ted and Peggy's funny offbeat friend.

Peggy approached Eliza, and with a little gesture indicating secrecy she exhibited her left hand, where above the wide gold band that she had worn for years (ten) now appeared a new green circle of stones. Peggy, with her reddish hair and large brown eyes, had a weakness for green, today a too bright (Eliza thought) green knit dress. But the ring was very pretty indeed; this was clear even to Eliza, whose lusts did not run toward jewelry. "Oh, that's so pretty," she said.

Peggy was terribly pleased; regarding her becoming new ring, she smiled but said, "Well, it's not too bad. I thought it was pretty nice, an anniversary present from the old boy." She had a tendency to speak of Ted in this way, in a good-fellow tone, which was odd to Eliza's ears, since she was sure that Peggy loved Ted. Ten years must mean love, mustn't it?

Eliza asked, "But is this an anniversary party, then? Peggy, why didn't you say?"

"Oh, well, we didn't want to advertise. You know, presents and all that jazz." Further proof to Eliza of the true intimacy of the Kennerlies; theirs was a private love.

And how did she, Eliza, really feel about this marriage, this successful love? At various times she had asked herself this question, and had come up with a variety of opposing reactions: pleasure, envy, boredom, disbelief. But she was fond of Peggy, on the whole.

Peggy laughed—her style included a lot of warm, small and inexplicable laughter, and she asked, "Well, tell me, what do you think of him?"

"Who?" She was, of course, pretending.

"Harry Argent, of course. Ted thinks he's pretty terrific, really successful, and he certainly is attractive, don't you think? Of course I guess he's not exactly your type."

"Do I have a type? I thought I was just promiscuous."

"Oh, Eliza, what a thing—how can you say that?" Peggy laughed.

"Anyway, what does he do, Mr. Argent?"

"He's in movies—of course not an actor. He's obviously too bright for that. He produces them. Ted says he has tons of money. And some he's even written and directed." Peggy named a couple of movies that Eliza thought she had heard of, had not seen.

"Well, if he's so terrific maybe I'll run away with him. We'll elope," said Eliza.

Peggy laughed again, and moved away.

Eliza began to talk to some other people who were near her elbow, people whom she had met before and almost forgotten. They were talking about skiing, which is what they all had done the previous weekend, at Sugar Bowl. And Eliza, who did not ski, imagined white spaces of snow, and frozen blue lakes, as vividly as she had earlier pictured hot beaches in Mexico.

In fact, the huge windows of that expensive house were lashed with rain, rattled with violent and unremitting wind. It was a winter storm that seemed to promise to remain forever, with no warmth or light, no spring.

Someone was saying, "The intro could just be a shot of that window, with water streaking down it, and the clouds. Some heads bobbing around in this room, giving the sense of a party. Party clothes, animated faces. And then after the titles and credits, all that junk, a cut to the beach at Ixtapanejo. Plane trips are all the same, unless you crash, and that's a kind of exploitation film that doesn't interest me. Any more. Anyway, the beach—and a couple lying there alone in the sun. Who've just made love. Or maybe not—that would be up to you." And Harry Argent, who was speaking from Eliza's other, non-ski-talk elbow, looked at her with a sort of friendly inquiry.

Everything about him was so outrageous that she laughed, but at the same time she was glad to see him back.

He took her arm and guided her expertly between people and furniture to a corner near the window; he asked, "No draft? You won't be cold here? Well, tell me a little about yourself. Just a little, really. I'm not a good listener. You know, your current status, aside from being unemployed."

"I'm divorced." She always said this. Never: I'm a widow.

Impatiently he said, "Of course you are. Divorced. Only interesting if you'd done it five or six times, and at your age that's pretty unlikely. Any kids?"

"One. Catherine. She's ten."

He was quick to say, "We could take her along. That would be a whole other trip. It might be interesting."

"At the moment she's in Boston, with my mother. Spring vacation. At her school what they call a ski break."

"Jesus, a ski break. Some schools these days." Berlin had become heavier in his voice.

"Oh, well, it's probably simpler this way. Two people. Grownups."

"Look." Eliza faced him and laughed. "You can't possibly think I'm coming to Mexico with you? To some preposterous town I've never heard of?"

"Well, why not? Look," he said to her, "I'm not divorced, not quite, and my wife has been giving me a pretty hard time. I'd like to talk to a pretty, intelligent girl who has an imagination. I can see all that in you; I have an infallible instinct for friends, unfortunately not for wives. And I talk best on beaches, and Ixtapanejo is not preposterous. It's there, and it's really beautiful."

* * *

"Plane trips are all the same, unless you crash." This sentence revolved in Eliza's hollowed head as the plane lurched, jolted sideways, and, beside her, Harry Argent peacefully slept, smiling slightly at whatever vision occupied his sleeping mind. And Eliza thought how strange that she should die with a man she didn't know at all.

For distraction she concentrated on the two people across the aisle: an almost middle-aged and getting-fat couple, in cheap and garish Hollywood clothes; sleepily affectionate with each other, they exchanged words in accents that Eliza believed to be Australian. But what were they doing in those clothes, why going to Acapulco? What in life did they do? And why were they not afraid? Why was she the only person on the plane in such a state of panic?

Seen from the air, at dawn, even Acapulco was beautiful: the lovely white curve of coast, the pink-tinged new tall hotels.

"Actually it's a cesspool, one of the ugliest places in the world," Harry muttered to Eliza as they landed, as she unclenched her stiff fingers from the sides of the seat.

They went through customs easily; no one would search Harry's voluminous and overweight pale leather fitted suitcase, or Eliza's overnight bag, which she had pulled together in the ten minutes allowed her by Harry between departing from the Kennerlies' party and going to the airport.

And then, outside the baggage room, Harry left her to stand in the palmy sultry day—to wonder why and where she was—while he went off to see about renting a car.

Returned, "It's the only car available," he said disconsolately. It was a long maroon Cadillac, whose young Mexican driver was uniformed in beige.

Having imagined a Fiat, or a VW, Eliza wondered just what he had wanted. Later she asked, "What kind of car do you usually drive?" "Uh—I have several. Mostly English." "Oh."

. . .

Sometimes, during that drive to Ixtapanejo (a name that she never learned to spell), Eliza slept, and then at intervals she woke to find herself in the midst of improbably towering palm trees, of forests of palm. Passing tiny huts of plaster or brick, roofs thatched or made of crude tile, sometimes with crude porches instead of a front wall. She tried then, and totally failed, to imagine the lives in those houses.

This was the same effort that her sister Daria made, driving among the poor of Southern Europe, in the outskirts of Naples or Rome—an imaginative effort that nearly broke her.

They were sitting on a balcony—their own, small and private—overlooking some tropical abundance of flowers, of greenery, and the wide white beach, the sea and an extraordinary pink-to-mackerel sunset. Sitting with long drinks, having spent the afternoon in the clear green warmish water, on the beach, having bathed, having made love.

Harry was saying, "It's too gorgeously romantic, isn't it? No one would believe it for a minute. It's like those travelogues when we were kids, remember? No, you're too young. 'And so we say farewell'—they used to end like that, always with improbable sunsets."

Eliza had just understood that he was again writing, seeing a movie of his own.

"On the other hand," he went on, "why not? Why not an old-fashioned extravaganza, Janet Gaynor watching Fredric March as he goes off to drown in the sunset—why not?" And he stared morosely at the actual sunset before them, perhaps not seeing it.

Eliza was thinking, I am drowned in sensation, I may never surface. And she smiled vaguely, exhaustedly.

Viewed analytically (which was not, at the moment, how she was viewing it), what was astonishing about their making love was Harry's apparent total disregard for his own pleasure.

Eliza had never known anything like it, such a minute and loving attention to her body. Inexperienced in that way, and concerned for him, she held back, until from somewhere she heard him say, "Go on—I can feel everything that you feel—"

Now Harry reached and took her hand—was this a part of his movie? He said, "You're a lovely woman." And he sighed. "If I had any sense at all, I'd marry you tomorrow."

She bridled a little at that—of course. "You assume that I want to get married?"

He looked at her. "Actually not. You're an original, I can tell. A sort of *zaftig* Jane Fonda, or Kim Novak with brains." He laughed. "You see? I can't even cast you, much less marry you." And then again he sighed. "Anyway, I only marry mean thin women, ones who will get old and look a lot like Judith Anderson."

Breakfast was a buffet: a beautiful array of fresh fruits, pineapples and mangoes and melons and bananas. Fresh warm moist tortillas and cold bacon.

And the dining room was open to the tropical luxuriance that surrounded it, the palms and bougainvillaea, the fresh new morning breeze from far out at sea.

Harry was saying, "It's interesting—when women really hate you, they refuse to divorce you. Ever noticed? You'd think they'd welcome a settlement. I'm honestly not mean about money. Good riddance, you'd think they'd say. But no, I'll never let you go—that's what they say. Eliza, what would you do if you could do anything you wanted?"

"I'd write really good poetry." Saying this, Eliza noted that she had not said it to anyone before, and she thought, How odd, I hardly know him—and she smiled at that.

"Really." He stared across the table at her, with those pale and intense blue eyes, as she imagined, or sensed, that he was imagining a movie about a woman poet. Jane Fonda?

And then, pointing to somewhere behind her back, to the gigantic screen of palms, he said, "Look! there's a macaw—a real one!"

Around noon, as they sat beneath the small round circular thatched roof, thus sheltered from the overwhelming sun, Harry decided, or said, that actually, really, they should get married. "The point is that I *like* you," he said violently to Eliza. "You're *nice*. Intelligent. Original. You're *kind*, or so far you seem to be a kind woman."

Mildly embarrassed, she laughed. "Sometimes I am," she said.

He wasn't really listening to what she said, and it occurred to Eliza that this was to be another movie. *(The Proposal? Marriage?)*

"I've never been married to a woman I liked," said Harry. "Isn't that terrible? Christ, it would be *marvelous*."

Earlier they had been swimming in the clear warm mild green surf. A converted Californian, Harry was adept at taking waves; some instinct informed him of the precise moment in the rise and breaking of a wave when he should plunge into it, swim and then let himself be hurled toward the shore. Eliza at first watched nervously; his shoulders were thin, and what he did looked dangerous, and sometimes there were long moments before he surfaced. Then she understood that he was an expert, and she stopped watching and swam, and swam and swam, thinking hazily of Maine, of hot days, swimming there.

And she was thinking less of Harry's notions of marriage than of the fact that she was terribly hungry.

They lunched adventurously in a shack on the beach in which a Mexican family served lobster and clams, broiled red snapper, all garlicky—marvelous. Cold beer.

Harry had begun to talk about a town in Italy where he owned (or did not own: this was unclear) a large house. Ravello.

"You'd be crazy about it," he said. "You know, the Amalfi coast. But up in the hills above. The views—terraces of olive trees. The wine. In fact, *Beat the Devil* was shot there, remember?"

She remembered Peter Lorre, John Huston—she thought Gina Lollobrigida—whoever. Not views, or a town.

"Well, anyway," he told her, "you'll love it there. I've never had an Italian honeymoon, have you?"

(Italian Honeymoon?)

After lunch they swam again, they lay in the sun, moved on to shade. They went back to their room and made love and slept and made love again.

It was absolutely incredible, all of it. Eliza literally could not credit what was happening, in the luxuriantly blooming, green-flowing, impossibly beautiful place.

At some moment—perhaps it was the next day while Eliza was watching the sunset: she was alone, Harry on some violent and unexplained impulse having summoned a taxi and gone into the small town—at that moment an idea entered her mind, or, rather, a sentence: Well, why not—why not marry Harry? And she smiled, because it sounded as silly as it was improbable. But that silly sentence, having been spoken within her brain, stayed there, and from time to time she heard its echo.

Harry came back, running into the room, seeming to have run down all the steps from the entranceway; he was carrying a large and curiously wrapped package, apparently not heavy. He threw it lightly onto the bed, toward Eliza, who had come in from the terrace at the sound of his footsteps.

"Open it, it's your first present from me!" He was breathless and perspiring; he put his hands on his narrow hips, leaning back and watching her, so visibly pleased with himself, and with her.

She undid a clumsy knot, pulled back paper, and there were half a dozen bright shades of cotton: crisp long dresses, all pleated and laced. A butterfly swarm of dresses.

Unreasonably moved, Eliza said, "Harry—" It seemed suddenly odd to use his name. "These are wonderful, I *love* them."

He had been watching her closely, and now he spoke seriously. "You're better at giving things, aren't you? Receiving makes you just a little nervous? Well, no matter. You'll learn."

She put on a yellow dress, with white insets of lace across her now brown breasts. Barefoot and laughing, they went up to the bar for their pre-dinner margaritas.

"This vogue for the realistic film can't last, you know? God knows what's next, some sort of nostalgia, probably. And then if things get really bad we'll go back to romance, the extravagant escape. And then, baby, I'll be right there—there first, with the most romantic, most extravagant film they've ever seen." Harry gestured into the starry air.

The bar was an open platform, set out from the main part of the hotel. Eliza and Harry were in adjoining chairs near the railing, overlooking the sea—looking out into the star-feathered night. They were holding hands. (Why should they not marry?)

At dinner, in the dining room, they did not talk about marriage, or, really, about movies. They had two bottles of wine; they observed the other guests, they talked and laughed a lot.

The hotel's owner-manager, Otto, was a pale and cadaverous German, perpetually worried. "Do you know who he looks like?" Harry asked. "Like Alec Guinness playing the German owner of a Mexican resort hotel."

Perfect.

Marrying Harry, *really*, would be no less sensible than coming to Mexico with him—a then unknown man, Eliza dreamily thought. It was about noon on the next day, on the beach—their last day. Money, houses in Connecticut and Italy and southern California. No more stupid jobs and worries about paying schools and dentists and department stores. No more frightening trips to unemployment. Great sex. And Harry was a genuinely nice man, intelligent and kind, a man for whom by then she felt a genuine affection. Much nicer than the men with whom she had been "in love." Why, after all, did people marry?

A morning of swimming and sun, and then they were again beneath the small thatched shelter. Harry had put a towel across his thin knees, which were reddening dangerously. He yawned, and said, "Tell me more about your mother, and your sister. Josephine and Daria? I do want to know, and it will be a good lesson in listening for me."

Eliza found that mildly irritating, but dutifully she began with Josephine, listing her books, enumerating awards—her fame. Her three husbands. And then Daria: her beauty, her delicacy. Her marriage last August to Smith Worthington, the wedding, the trip to Europe, the worrying, sad letters—but then her pregnancy, and their projected move to Woodside this coming summer, after the baby was born.

Harry's eyes were closed. In repose, his facial muscles slack, the lines on either side of his face were deeper, as though from suffering. Was it possible that Eliza had just noticed those dark furrows? After all, they hardly knew each other. Of herself, she observed, somewhat curiously, that she was relieved by his apparent inattention; in some way she had not wanted to tell him about Josephine and Daria.

But he opened his eyes, and at once he was totally in focus, in control. He said, "I think you worry too much about your sister. She may be delicate and vulnerable, but how can you protect her?" And, as Eliza was digesting that, he went on: "You have no idea how your voice changes, going from your mother to your sister. From stiff to warm. Your mother really scared you, a long time back?"

Eliza could not believe that she had said all that; he had

understood too much. It was a sort of invasion. (But was that a good reason not to marry someone, that he understood you too well? It may well be, from time to time she thought.)

Their last sunset was the most fantastic, most gorgeous one of all: violently ragged mackerel clouds adorned the sky, which slowly, majestically darkened to purple, then faded to a pale and delicate lavender, in which suddenly faint stars appeared, like flowers.

"You're the kindest, most interesting woman I've ever met," Harry said. "All your tastes are lovely. We *must* get married. Think what a great time we could have."

She did think of it. She said, "Well, maybe you're right. Maybe we should. Get married," and she laughed a little breathlessly.

He reached and grasped her neck, pulling her toward him; they kissed, and then he laughed. *"A Sudden Marriage,"* he said. "How about that? Starting just as we did, at that silly pretentious party at your friends' house. The Kennedys. Kennerlies? And then coming here. But I'm absolutely serious. Are you?"

She looked at him. They were at the bar, again seated near the railing, near the sky. She said yes.

They had a glorious night of celebration—wine and laughing and love.

The next morning, at breakfast, and as they came back to the room to pack, Harry's mood was still festive—exuberant: he was whistling dance tunes from his youth: "Tuxedo Junction," "Little Brown Jug" and "Someone Exactly Like You." And then he sang, in a funny hoarse tremolo, "I dreamed of two blue orchids, two beautiful blue orchids last night—"

Whereas Eliza was tense, grasped by her familiar pre-flying panic. This time, she thought, of course they were going to crash. Just when her life had settled—just when, as Smith, her brother-in-law, would put it, she was becoming "appropriate." She was not supposed to marry a kind and loving, intelligent man, who was also extremely rich. Of course the plane will crash.

On the plane Eliza had several vodkas, which helped. The air was clear and blue, was beautiful! And below was the beautiful blue sea, the smooth Pacific.

Harry was talking excitedly about his movie—one of his movies. "And then in Italy," he said, "the fantastic honeymoon. Driving through Umbria in a Bentley, in the spring. As I see it, we marry in a month or so? Do you want more children? No? good. I can get everything squared away by May. There are red flowers all over the hillsides then. My favorite restaurant is in a town called Todi. It's called The Umbria, in fact. You'll love it."

He seemed now not to be talking about a movie at all but about an actual marriage—theirs. And in a vague but excited way Eliza was able to see it—to share, as it were, his vision.

She saw them on the terrace of a restaurant, looking out to a distance of Umbrian hills, gently sloped and terraced—to fields of tiny flowers, yellow and red. The clarity with which she saw this was remarkable, as she had never been to Italy.

And they are married. Happy. Rich, and safe. (Appropriate.)

But Eliza and Harry did not marry, and the only fantasy to be realized, ever, was Harry's movie.

What happened at first was a literal drift apart. Suddenly Harry had to be on location in Morocco, and Eliza, because of Catherine's school (and really because she couldn't afford it; she could neither pay for such a trip nor bring herself to ask him for the money), Eliza could not join him there. Weeks passed, with impassioned transatlantic calls, and then a frantic weekend rendezvous in New York, which did not go well.

9 / Bad News from All Over

Always, on the every other Tuesdays that were unemployment days, Eliza woke up too early. Her nerves were raw, and her mind apprehensive, darkly polluted by fears and stained with elusive bad dreams. Fears and guilts, her demons without names, with only tattered and sooty shapes. She tried to go back to sleep—eyes closed, body forced to relax; and she failed.

Instead, her uncontrolled imagination explored the vivid murky alleys in the vicinity of Third and Bryant, near the unemployment building, a giant cube of pale green peeling plaster. Seedy bars, menacing loiterers. It was as though all the mounting violence of the city centered there, in her mind, although she knew this to be untrue.

Recognizing that she was not going back to sleep, she opened her eyes and tried to name or to sort out her fears. One, she was afraid of being mugged—knifed, beaten, hurt. And two, she was afraid of losing the money. Losing it to a mugger—or, a less violent, more guilty fear, she could be denied the payment. Some faceless person behind the counter could decide that she did not deserve unemployment money (was this her own view?), would *know* that she had not seriously looked for work. They would think that she did not need the money, would take Miriam's view of her, that she was rich.

But she was not rich, she did need the money. And her fears were disproportionate; she knew that.

She knew, too, that she had always overreacted to everything; very likely she always would. Wasn't poetry itself an overreaction to experience?

She got out of bed and, dressing, she dropped things. Her jeans zipper stuck.

At breakfast she was cross with Catherine, who banged out of the house.

And then, in the paper, Eliza read:

> The body of a young black woman, who had been shot in the head at close range, was discovered this morning by early strollers on Ocean Beach. Darryl Evans, 36, and Horace Crane, both of Lincoln Way, came upon the corpse, which was half buried in the sand across from Playland-at-the-Beach. The victim was described as being in her late teens or early twenties, very dark complexion . . .

Trembling, Eliza dialed Miriam's number; also, of course, Miriam's mother's number. Busy, busy. Busy for twenty minutes.

Panicked, Eliza telephoned Kathleen at the hospital office.

"Kathleen, it's Eliza, did you read in the paper—is Miriam there?"

"No, she's not, and yes, I did read it. Of course it could be her. Dumb black bitch, always messing around. I've told her—"

But Eliza was unable to listen, today, to Kathleen's raging. monologue.

And it was time to go to unemployment. On her way out she dialed Miriam. Still busy.

That day, in the huge, hangar-like, dreary greenish room, (called, euphemistically, the Office of Human Resources Development), in the unemployment lines, everyone looked like

Miriam. The room was full of tall black girls with skinny legs, hunched over in their coats. But why would Miriam be here? She was almost anywhere else. Or dead.

And Eliza's head was raw with sleeplessness.

Sometimes, perhaps because of the weather, there was unreasonably a sort of festive atmosphere in that room, up and down the waiting lines. Kids in bright crazy clothes, tall black men with terrific swaggering hats, all getting something for nothing. Sometimes it felt childish and fun.

But not today. Today the kids looked pale and shabby, the black men dangerous.

And this was Eliza's interview day; about every six weeks the unemployment recipients had to say where they had applied for jobs. Possibly Eliza was not the only person who was not really looking for a job; possibly other people did as she did, which was to make up a few plausible places. (Miriam's instructions: "List some folks you know. Like that, if they check you, you be okay.") She listed Ted Kennerlie, sometimes The Lawyer. Still, she was always terrified of being somehow found out.

But her system worked, her small deception. The efficient-looking young Japanese man on the other side of the railing barely glanced at her list. He handed her her check, as once more she caught a glimpse of a black girl across the room, who was not Miriam.

She took the check to the office next door, where it had to be exchanged for cash: more danger. She headed for the bus stop across the street, afraid of everyone, of everything.

Miriam.

At home, with her coat still on, she picked up the phone and dialed, and Miriam answered on the first ring. "Hey, there, Eliza, how're you doing? You okay? *I'm* okay, *real* okay—"

The departure of Eliza's terror left her weak, too weak for anger; she felt shriveled, and suddenly small.

She said, "Well, I just wondered how you were—" and she

hung up, thinking, But it could have been Miriam; Miriam's life is dangerous. She is endangered; we all are, but especially Miriam. (We are not human resources.)

Half an hour later, Peggy Kennerlie called. She said that Ted was behaving strangely: he was talking about joining the Peace Corps.

Already bored, Eliza felt disloyal both to Peggy and to the Peace Corps. Peggy sounded ridiculous.

But not so, of course, to Peggy herself, who said, "I'm really worried, Liza" (an old college nickname that Eliza very much disliked). "It's so unlike him. But I guess it beats chasing his secretary."

"I guess so." As she said this, Eliza had a clear and certain vision that that would be next: Ted would dump Peggy for his secretary, especially if he had a virgin secretary. Ted as a sexual person would only be convincing to a virgin.

"Well, what do you hear from old Harry?" Peggy asked.

"Nothing. Nothing at all." Eliza sounded more irritated than she meant to, and for that she could not fairly blame Peggy.

The truth was she had not heard from "old Harry" since the weekend, almost a month ago now, when she flew to meet him in New York; and Peggy's question reminded her of what now seemed another failure in love—in love, or perhaps simply in judgment. How crazy to go off to Mexico with a man you didn't know, and even to imagine that you loved him, to think of marrying him. (How crazy to have married Evan Quarles.)

What did happen with Harry in New York? She had tried, with not much success, to sort that out. For a start, a bad start, they were both very tired, Harry from filming—a strenuous schedule—in Morocco, and then the trip, jet lag. Eliza was simply tired, for no reason. And the city, New York, seemed to conspire against them; everywhere, despite reservations, despite Harry's flamboyant force, they had to wait for meals. For taxis, for theatre tickets. Harry's joke was "Maybe we can only function in hyper-efficient Mexico," but Eliza feared that this was indeed the case.

Worse, as the weekend went on, she feared that she had built up Harry in her mind as a kind of super and hitherto inexperienced combination lover and friend. She had even (Christ! embarrassing to remember) brought along a couple of poems that she had been working on for him to see. And no possible moment for poems ever arrived.

By the end of the weekend, Harry's fatigue had evolved into a ferocious cold. They spent Sunday afternoon in bed, not making love (not reading poetry). Harry was coughing and blowing his nose with great violence; Eliza gloomily thinking.

But she had found it hard, somehow, to write off Harry. He would not become, in her mind, The Hollywood Producer, would not join The Consul and The Lawyer. To think of him was a further depressant, on a dark depressing day.

And that night Daria telephoned. She seemed to be crying, or barely succeeding in not crying. "I really feel okay," she said, "but I have to stay in bed for a while, and it is disappointing. We'd really wanted—"

She had had a miscarriage.

"Oh, Daria—Christ, I'm so sorry. But you know, you are so young."

"I know, sure, we can go on and have eleven children. But I wanted to have this one."

10 / *And Some Good News*

On a classically lovely day in early June, a Wednesday—
the day after an unemployment appointment that was less
frightening than usual—Eliza went down the slate steps to her
mailbox, about midmorning. She found there mostly bills and
advertisements, as usual. Macy's, Saks, Catherine's dentist. A
mail order catalogue, some fliers from magazines soliciting
subscriptions.

Retrieved and spread out on her coffee table, the array of
envelopes was discouraging: there was nothing among them to
read. Which meant no respite or postponement of work, from
either messy old unfinished poems or the perfectly blank paper
on her desk upstairs. Idly and without hope, she looked at all
those envelopes, and then, with a small rise of irritation, she
thought, I *subscribe* to the *Nation;* why are they writing?

Inside the *Nation* envelope was a short and graceful note:
"We are accepting, with particular pleasure, your poem . . . an
early issue . . . twelve dollars."

Involuntarily, in disbelief, Eliza's hands flew up to cover
her mouth as she stared at the small and important piece of
paper. And then happiness like new blood flooded through all
her veins. It was a moment of pure joy; she recognized and
greeted it as such, looking out to the pale blue spring sky, the
fluttering gray-green eucalyptus leaves, and much farther away

the rising wrinkled green hills of Marin County. Pure joy, and a moment that she would remember, would recapture, resee.

And now—whom to tell—to call?

Catherine was in school. Daria was in Italy, recuperating from her miscarriage. Harry Argent was in Morocco again, and she had no current lover.

Josephine? At the thought of phoning her mother and telling her this news, the familiar web of emotions began to knot and tangle in her chest: fear, guilt, affection, apprehension, anger. She dialed the well-known number: the house in Maine, which Josephine had gone to open for the summer.

The phone rang and rang, while Eliza pictured the house perfectly: the large rooms, long windows looking out to the June-sparkling lake, or, on the other side, back to the pale and green leafed-out apple trees. She could even smell that slight odor of disuse—perhaps less an odor than a need of air—that came from a neglected, although immaculately clean and polished house at the start of summer.

"Darling!" said Josephine, "how lovely to hear from you, such a surprise. And not calling collect!" She was out of breath, but insistently conversational. "What time of day is it out there? I can never remember which way it goes."

Not saying: I haven't called you collect for at least ten years (although knowing that she will say this, in her mind, to Josephine, repeatedly; she is fated to such unspoken fights with her mother), Eliza said, "It's eleven-fifteen. Mother, I have some really good news." And Eliza told her the news.

"Oh, Eliza, how marvelous! I'm absolutely delighted for you. But you didn't say that you'd been writing poetry."

"Well, it sounds sort of silly."

"Not silly at all, when you impress a magazine like the *New Republic*."

"The *Nation*, Mother."

"Oh, I meant the *Nation*. It's like the problem I used to have: no one could remember whether I had a piece in *Harper's* or the *Atlantic*. Darling, I am so glad you called. I had a card from Daria this morning. They're in Florence, and she seems to be feeling enormously better."

"Oh good."

"Well, I did think Italy would help. And they do seem to do it in style. I must say that Smith has rather grand notions." And then, unfortunately in the same breath, she asked, "How much do they pay for poetry? The *Nation*, right?"

"Right. Oh, not much. In fact, not much at all. I may take Catherine out for a Chinese lunch, or something."

"Oh, well, money."

That's easy for you to say: Eliza prevented herself from saying this to her mother, who had always earned a lot of money writing, and had inherited a lot. But she eerily recalled Smith Worthington saying those words to her, last summer in Maine, on the night before his marriage. "Mother, I have to go now," she lied. "I have a lunch. I just wanted to tell you—"

"Darling, I'm so glad—how good you were to call." And then Josephine's voice sounded tremulous: was that because they were saying goodbye, or because she was truly glad for Eliza's poem?

As she hung up, Eliza was trembling, and she did not understand, *really*, what had happened—or she could not face what she seemed to understand. Which was that Josephine was not entirely pleased.

An hour or so later, as she sat on her worn wooden front steps, in the sun, Eliza almost managed to return to her moment of joy. Smelling lavender, she thought of the enormous difference between having sold even one small poem and not. Being a published poet or not.

She wished that she were, in fact, meeting someone for lunch, but she did not have the right friend for that moment, and besides, it was too late—after noon.

Harry, if he were there—Harry would have been terrific, but he would have overdone it. Lunch at the Palace, champagne—he would have overwhelmed the event, and thus, not meaning to, have minimized it. Still, it would have been more fun with him.

And she thought of the splendid weekend that had succeeded the not good one in New York. Harry had had to come back to Los Angeles to look at rushes, and he managed three days on Nob Hill, at the Huntington—to which Eliza rushed for long afternoons of wine and love, some tiny naps—rushed home for supper with Catherine, back to Harry for more love and midnight feasts.

After that visit, Eliza thought, Well, he's marvelous, but I couldn't see him very often; I wouldn't last.

Inside, she considered calling Miriam, but that was crazy, too much to explain. Considered, and dismissed, Kathleen.

She even thought of calling Peggy Kennerlie.

And then she saw a possibly oncoming wave of self-pity, against which she firmly braced herself. Firmly she spread her competent hands before her on the table, and she thought, Of course it would not be as important to anyone else; no one else has been inside my head, feeling my craving for any recognition, my really dying to be published.

She said to herself, I send poems out into space; that's how it feels. And so, how extraordinary that someone should have heard. Someone bought my poem.

The threatened wave of self-pity did not strike.

The phone rang. It was Josephine, who said, in a hurried, out-of-character voice, "I just called because I wasn't sure I'd said how really glad I was. Just surprised. I wouldn't have thought of you as being a poet. But, darling, that's absolutely terrific. First-rate." Was Josephine crying? "Well, I must hang up. We don't want to start supporting the phone company, do we?"

Her daughter was totally confused.

But Eliza had almost returned to her earlier euphoria, when she heard loud and unexpected feet pounding up the stairs. It was, of course, Catherine, but then—at lunchtime?

"Mom, don't you remember? There's a teachers' meeting, so we all got out early! I told you!" Blond and beaming, plump and almost twelve, Catherine burst into the room, trailing books and a favorite bedraggled pink wool cardigan.

"Oh, no, I did forget, but, Cat, I'm so glad. And guess what happened to me today." Eliza told Catherine her news.

"Oh, Mom, a poem in a real magazine with your name on it? Mom, that's terrific—God, that's wonderful!"

Eliza and Catherine went off to Chinatown to have lunch, to celebrate.

11 / Expensive Hotels

What would it be like to be that woman? What goes on in her mind, or beneath her skin? Daria is thinking these questions as she stares at a youngish, black-wrapped, emaciated woman of indeterminate nationality—as they both stare down into an enclosed space of broken ruins. This is the Largo Argentina, in Rome, all overgrown with bright and thriving weeds, and overrun with cats: large and small, all colors, but uniformly scraggly cats, pirates, marauders; they sleep with one eye half open, one torn ear half cocked. Daria and the other woman are both watching the cats, but why? And what is she thinking and feeling, that other?

Poor: she is obviously very poor. The black clothes are rags, and both brown shoes gape open to dingy black socks, below a short space of bare raw white legs. Blond hair makes her look not Italian; her hair is the color of Daria's sister Eliza's hair, but otherwise, my God—how different the two. Daria imagines that she, the other, has wandered down to Italy from some other country—Poland? Austria?—maybe looking for work, a husband, a supportive relative. And nothing has worked out for her.

The woman turns to Daria and smiles, showing terrible teeth, and gestures toward the cats; she says something in her own language, which Daria partially understands; she has said, ". . . spaghetti."

And Daria turns to see that a reasonably well-dressed older man, perhaps a retired civil servant, in proper brown, has gone halfway down some steps and has set out a large platter of obviously cold and old spaghetti. Which several dozen cats gobble down in half an instant. The plate now is perfectly clean, as its owner retrieves it. He is smiling to himself, as though this were a favorite moment of his day.

Ashamed of her own perfect, expensively maintained teeth, excruciatingly aware of expensive, impractical clothes, Daria smiles guardedly at the other woman. (After all, they have the cats in common.) And she thinks, I will give her all my money.

Will becomes *must*, an absolute imperative. It has the force of a superstition, or a charm. Since she had that thought—that directive, as it were—she must obey it.

She is to meet her husband—"Smith Worthington, my husband"—for lunch in a place called the Casina Valadier. "It's up on the Pincio; you'll have to take a cab. Just remember the name—here, I'll write it on a card." On one side engraved "SMITH WORTHINGTON," on the other, tidily printed in ink, "Casina Valadier." "And here, you might see something you want—" She is handed a sheaf of lire, crisp pale notes. "Oh, well, you might need more." More notes. "Don't spend it all in one place." He laughs.

She has no idea how much money there is, no idea of the worth of all those notes, those large-denominated lire, folded inside her suede kid-lined bag. No matter; in fact, it is probably better not to know. Daria has been indulgently told for a long time that she has no head for figures: first by her astronomy professor at college, a kindly Dutchman; and later by her husband. But there are certain numbers that she remembers as secrets: for example, six million. Hitler killed six million Jews. And why does she remember this number, why think of it now, what happened when she was a small child? (This is in the middle Sixties, by which time Smith has made five million dollars and Daria has had four miscarriages; she does not think of these facts, neither being as real to her as six million Jews, dead.) She does think, Last night he fucked me four times—"Fuck," a secret word that no one knows she uses in her thoughts, certainly not Smith, the exhaustedly proud fucker.

Fucking: Daria senses that this is something that Smith must do; he must drive himself into her, as untouchingly and as often as possible. Often—that is very important to Smith. He counts; she has heard him mutter to himself, "Twice a night for a week, that's pretty good for an old guy pushing thirty."

No matter, then, the amount, the numbers of the money. The essential, the necessary thing is to give it all, and then to run away. Daria stares around at the streets that bound the small square, streets thunderous with the tearing traffic of an approaching Roman noon: heavy buses, darting urgent cars, careening delivery bicycles and roaring motorcycles. No exit. She will have to rush through the traffic, praying Roman prayers. Santa Sophia? Minerva? Agatha?

Now she moves along the railing toward the other woman—the other, the poor and unlucky. She is holding her bag in a way that feels furtive and embarrassed. And she feels embarrassed perspiration seeping under her arms, down her dark silk dress.

Up close, the woman looks older, worse. Cracked pale lips, a white flaking around her nostrils, red-rimmed eyes. Still, at a certain time she was a young woman, obviously. A blond young woman with breasts, and everything, all invisible now beneath rags. Men wanted to fuck her. How did she feel about that—that "fucking"?

With the most rapid gesture she can manage (her hands shake a little; the tight new clasp of her bag resists), Daria reaches inside the bag; trying to cover what is now in her hand (impossible, such large bills), she thrusts it toward the woman, and says (unaccountably) in French: *"C'est pour vous. Un petit cadeau—moi—"* She turns then and begins to run, before there has been any change of expression on that other face. Any word, in whatever language.

If she is killed, run over by a hurtling Porsche, with Smith Worthington's impressive card in her bag, and if the ragged woman is found in the area with a lot of money, the police will piece together robbery, blackmail, something terrible. This worries Daria as she runs, dodging cars; but she is too busy not getting killed, not wanting to die just now, in Rome, near noon, when she is supposed to be meeting Smith for lunch.

Her fashionable shoes are low, small-heeled, but new and tight. Having made it across the street, a miracle, Daria slows down a little, although continuing to walk rapidly: a beautiful dark American (half Greek, but that is hard to tell), a fragile girl who looks as though she knows where she is going—who does not dare to turn around.

And then suddenly before her is a huge rounded gray stone shape, recognizable as the Pantheon. They have been there, she and Smith; they have "done" it, put money in and listened from earphones to recorded history. But what Daria remembers is the cool, the dizzying rise of space up to the dome. Mainly the cool—and so she goes inside.

For the first time, it occurs to her that having done what she was in effect told to do, what she *meant* to do, she has no money. The imperative did not allow for holding back a few hundred lire, calculating cab costs. Daria is thinking of this as she watches the door, and sees other people coming in. They are tourists, like herself, or the native poor and reverent; no lost foreign woman is among them.

Daria is perfectly aware that she is supposed to be at the Casina Valadier to meet Smith Worthington in exactly twenty minutes; however, it does not seem urgent, in that ancient and soaring roundness, that cool gray.

In a certain predictable way, Smith will not mind either her lateness or her being out of money. Women *are* late, and they spend a lot of money, and they are shy about "fucking." All she has to do is to arrive, although late, a little breathless, with a powdered nose and smoothed hair, and no visible perspiration. A story about a jewelry shop on the Piazza Navona. A lovely cameo ring, on order. It is only the truth that would enrage him: "I was watching some cats, mangy hungry ones. I saw this woman, and I gave her— Well, what could I give her, cold spaghetti?"

The small restaurant, its terrace overlooking most of Rome, is very French: elegant and terribly expensive, even by inflated Roman standards. And excellent French food.

Smith is having his second perfect martini; Daria, just arrived, a vermouth cassis.

Her eyes are sad and gray, and Smith is remembering a magazine article he once read that contained a quiz for people who suppose themselves happily married: What color are your wife's eyes? This was among the questions. And he had thought, Of course, Daria's eyes are brown. But the next time he looked at her, examiningly, her eyes were a yellowy green, cat's eyes. And the next time gray, as now. In another article, another magazine somewhere, it said that people with variably colored eyes are especially prone to mental illness. He himself thinks, or at this moment he decides, that it is simply a question of light; the too bright light at noon in this white, white room has grayed Daria's eyes. Besides, she looks tired, almost drained. Traveling is sometimes hard on women.

To divert her, and to cheer them both, he says, "Well, I talked to New York this morning, and the market has really gone crazy this week. I mean, it's terrific. Guess how much money we made—just take a guess."

" . . . "

"Try. In one week. Just guess."

"Six million?" Raised gray eyes.

He laughs. "You're funny, you really are. Well, okay, not

quite that much. But would you believe—three hundred grand?"

"Three hundred grand?" She has managed to make the phrase sound foreign, even crazy.

He translates for them both. Three hundred thousand dollars, in one week.

"Oh." She sounds disappointed.

Rather wildly, he says, "And you'll never guess who Al is sure will run in '68." He says a name.

Startlingly, Daria says, "But didn't he lose to Kennedy in 1960, and make that terrible speech about not kicking him around any more?"

Her bursts of accuracy sink Smith's heart. Why is he most frightened when she is most reasonable? But he chooses to answer as though they were having a reasonable conversation. "You're absolutely right, of course," he says. "But really in politics it's anyone's guess."

However Daria has already lost interest in this exchange, and in a dull gray voice has begun to say, "I'm sorry I was so late, but I found this really lovely store, a window full of cameos, on the Piazza Navona, and I ordered—"

Later they go back to their hotel, above the Spanish Steps, back to their room with the wonderful view of Rome, and Smith fucks her twice. Two times.

In the suburb of some city, probably Naples, going to or perhaps away from the airport, their hired car breaks down. Smith and the driver go off somewhere to see about it, and Daria, perfectly safely, is left outside the small plaster wall, terribly painted blue, that surrounds a tiny geranium-decked house, also blue. It is a confrontation; Daria is confronted and challenged by that house. Who lives inside, and what is it like to live there?

The wooden doorstep is worn down, the lintel crooked.

Crisp red curtains flutter at the window. (What do they mean?) In the yard is an empty clothesline, a broken wheelbarrow. Is the house, then, abandoned, or are its people simply out shopping, to return momentarily? Are they the recent victims of calamity, some accident, all now gathered around a bed in some nearby hospital?

What does that house mean?

When Smith and the driver come back to the car, bringing a mechanic who fixes it in five minutes, Daria is weeping in the back seat, at the failure of her imagination.

In Paris, Daria gives away—"loses" is the explanation for Smith; she is tired of inventing jewelry that will never arrive— lovely new francs amounting to about nine hundred dollars, Smith says. Nine thousand—ninety? It is hard to be sure.

And again the money is given to an old woman, ragged and poor. "Has it occurred to you that in some way you are placating your mother, Josephine?" one of Daria's eventual psychiatrists will ask. No, Daria will want to say; how could a poor woman remind me of strong and successful Josephine? It's just that old women look poorer than anyone; it's just that I am a woman. The ragged old women remind me of myself. But she will not say this. Why bother?

An international conference having to do with money is going on at the Amstel, in Amsterdam; that is why Daria and Smith are there. It is their final expensive hotel. In the corridors and the elevators are those worried and highly specialized men, pale and serious and sexless, dark, heavy with inside informa- tion. Daria finds them frightening, and she dislikes that massive gray hotel, a fortress, piled up on the banks of the wide canal.

She escapes to walk alone beside other, smaller canals. This is all right. Smith is extremely busy, and the city is quite safe.

It is early fall; in that cool northern seaport city, the leaves have begun to turn pale yellow. Arched stone bridges, cobbled sidewalks beside the narrow dark brick houses with long windows of gleaming glass. Storefronts displaying pewter and porcelain, wooden dolls, bread and cheese. In those streets nothing is dangerous but the veering bicycles, and those at least make no noise, no fumes. Walking, stopping to look and to breathe the fresh cool air that smells of leaves and of fall, Daria experiences a lightening of her spirits, and of her senses; it is like an experience of love. She feels safe and inconspicuous, beautifully alone.

Fat blond babies who look more Dutch than anyone smile up from comfortable prams; there seem to be no poor people. Some shabby students, yes, and even funny-looking American kids, boys with long hair (hippies, a word that Daria has not yet heard), but all animatedly talking. Not worrying to her.

No sad old women.

She *likes* Amsterdam; "love" is a word that Daria does not use when she can help it. She likes it better than anywhere she has ever been—except, possibly, Maine, that house. But Maine is too exciting, really disturbing, the thrilling dark wind-torn lake, sharp mountains and violent rotting smells of apples. Amsterdam is human-sealed, is peaceful.

And what a handsome couple they are, there in Amsterdam, she and Smith in the huge Amstel dining room. As though she were somewhere else in the room—were, perhaps, that small dark-blond man in the corner—Daria can see them, see herself and Smith. They are the lovely young couple at the important window table overlooking the terrace and the broad canal. Her cloudy winged hair, yellow eyes, her gray baroque pearls; his thick dark hair, white brow and wide brown eyes. She can see them clearly.

Daria is in a mood or perhaps a seizure of clairvoyance: she has described exactly what that young blond man in the corner, whose name is Reed Ashford, has seen, what he is seeing. She has seen his view of herself and Smith. He, Reed, has met Smith that afternoon; he would like to meet Smith's wife, and later on he will. He thinks she is lovely, the wife; she is rather like a woman in San Francisco (he lives there) with whom, at that time, he is much involved. A troubled young married woman, terribly in love with him. Daria is not so much like her as she is the same type, a dark cloudy wispy woman. His type.

Daria and Smith are having a surprisingly rational political discussion. Since Smith is a Republican and she disagrees with him, he has defined her as a Democrat, although Daria is not at all sure that she is that. What are you, if you dislike anything that is happening? She will have to ask Josephine, who will say, with a dismissing sort of laugh, "You must be an anarchist, my darling. A sort of Basque." But now, reasonably, Daria is saying, "When you say fiscal responsibility, it seems to me that you really mean rich people keeping their money." She clasps her long thin white fingers on the cleared table before her.

Across from her, Smith shudders very slightly. It has just flashed through his mind that he hates her hands; they remind him of white spiders, or something. He is afraid of her hands—but that is ridiculous. He loves Daria, his beautiful wife, her beautiful jeweled hands.

But Daria has seen, or felt, that hate-fear flash. She puts her hands in her lap, out of sight, and she stops listening to him.

Smith is saying, pleasantly, as he reaches for his pipe, "Well, of course, in a way you're right. I've worked hard for my money, *our* money, and I would certainly prefer to keep it. But suppose I didn't, suppose I gave it all away to charities tomorrow, do you really imagine that would improve the world?"

"—what?"

Daria has just had another view into Smith's mind, or perhaps it is a vision of a later Smith: this Smith of the future is a man with a terribly sick wife (who must be herself, Daria?), so sick that she cannot be touched, assuredly not fucked, but Smith is gentle and sadly faithful to her; he loves his sick wife, he loves being the husband of a sick wife. And she has to do nothing, nothing at all; it is an absolution.

"—very glad to meet you," the dark-blond young man is saying, now standing beside their table.

Daria smiles, and gives him one of her hands, which he takes as though it were something familiar to him, and he smiles, narrowing dark blue eyes, flashing white teeth—as Daria thinks of the lake in Maine: dangerous.

"Join us for a brandy?" Smith is saying affably; this man must be someone he likes, rich and successful, fiscally responsible.

"Delighted to, but I think not brandy. I've become addicted to the local lemonade," says Reed.

"What a wonderful idea," Daria says, in an unusually spontaneous way, so that they both smile gently in her direction; she is for the moment an indulged and pretty child.

They all have lemonade, and they talk about how much they like it here in Amsterdam.

Daria observes that this man, this Reed Ashford, actually has two faces: a flashing, dangerous, hard face, and another that is mild and passive, almost sweet. And she has a curious urge to tell this young man about her sister, about Eliza, of whom she is so proud. She projects a conversation in which she tells him about Eliza, her poetry in all those magazines. ("I doubt if Reed subscribes to the *New Republic,* or the *Partisan Review,*" Smith would say. "No, but I've heard of them, I even see them from time to time," would certainly be Reed's response. How she knows him!)

But at the moment that Daria is about to talk about Eliza, Reed looks dangerous again, although he is quite small—a small and perfect man—and so she does not.

He seems to like to talk about himself, this Reed, which could not be said of either Smith or Daria; they are rather charmed by his ingenuously confessional manner. Also, to them his background is exotic: Hollywood, his mother was a sometime movie star. Sally Ashford. Oh, yes, they remember her. Of course, he looks exactly like her, the lovely hollow cheeks and wide slant eyes.

"I can't imagine an unhealthier atmosphere for a kid," Reed says, looking very young. "As a result, I was crazy about the awful prep school they finally shipped me off to."

But he does not tell them the name of the school; after all, it wasn't Groton, not a famous place. And so they do not discover what is an extraordinary, quite sinister coincidence: Reed Ashford was the boy whom Evan Quarles fell fatally in love with.

(Told of this much later, Eliza's friend Harry Argent says, "Well, it's really not so amazing. You American Eastern prep school types all seem to find each other eventually, especially if you're anywhere near the same age." "Reed is five years younger than I am." "So? It's really a question of class." Harry sounds very Berlin as he says this, with harsh "r"s and flat vowels. He goes on, "But don't worry, I'd never use this plot for a film.")

It was a pleasant evening all around, for Daria and Smith and for Reed, in Amsterdam; and Reed was encouraged to visit them in Woodside. Telephone numbers were exchanged and noted down, time schedules given.

12 / Stopping Smoking

At some point in her middle thirties, Eliza, who for years had smoked a couple of packs a day, decided to stop. For every reason: health, and she disliked being addicted. Too, she saw that it was unpleasant for people who did not smoke. Harry, for example, a non-smoker, would be pleased at her not smoking.

She realized that she could only do it by stopping cold. And so she picked a day that was not far off, a day after which she would not smoke again.

She sat at her desk, in her pretty bedroom, not smoking but not working either; she was thinking only of cigarettes, craving one. Surely she could—only one? She tried to concentrate on the view, her prospect of sunny hills and streets, of bright water and slow ships, but she could hardly see.

Dull terrible sentences formed in her mind, such as: My life is not worth living. And she felt this to be true, she felt she had suffered a permanent loss.

But smoking doesn't, *really,* help a person write, she told herself.

She didn't smoke, and she continued, for weeks and months, to feel terrible: lost, deprived.

Sometimes, even, she cried, and then at other times she experienced a curious, unmotivated need to laugh; a hysteria that was later explained to her as being caused by an increase in oxygen.

Worst of all for her was the hour or so before dinner. Then, as she worked around the kitchen, making food for Catherine and herself, it all came down on her, all her feeling of failure and frustration, all the loneliness of her life. Soon Catherine would leave home, and then where would she be?

A strong part of her mind was aware that what she was going through was "withdrawal symptoms," like junkies have, and giving it that name was of some help. Still, her symptoms and everything in her mind were real; they were as real as names.

She got through the evenings with a lot of wine, although she had read that that was not a recommended course; still, it helped, and she treated herself to a case of good strong Italian peasant wine, from a North Beach delicatessen.

She found, too, that walking helped immensely, and she began to spend as much of her days as she could on walks. Covering the city. She took buses to remote areas, and then in those unfamiliar neighborhoods she walked, and walked. Mission Street: the multiplicity of South American groups, and cultures, the restaurants and stores all homogenized into something vaguely "Spanish," vaguely tawdry.

Or Potrero Hill: great bare spaces, wide streets, industrial views of San Francisco, and of the declining harbor.

Clement Street, with Russian, Greek or Chinese restaurants, delicatessens, used furniture, junk.

One afternoon, lured into a junk store by a display of antique earrings in the window, she found a small Victorian armchair; its ornate, deeply carved roses were all horribly varnished over. And it was probably for the sake of the horrible yellow varnish that she bought it, paid too much, and then more money for its delivery to Russian Hill. Stripping it—in fact, rescuing the wood—would take hours, and all her skill and strength.

. . .

But her virtue was not rewarded. After not hearing from Harry for a considerable while, this letter came:

> Well, I seem to have done it again, married a mean dark woman. This one is a Corsican, actually, and she will probably kill me. Eliza, it's all your fault, you should have married me that first time in Mexico.

An extremely—an *outrageously* depressing note. How could he? And Eliza's despair was made worse by her feeling that she had no right to it. Of course he could; he could do anything at all, and he had warned her of his tendencies toward marriage. They were classically uncommitted.

Now she couldn't, wouldn't see Harry, and she couldn't help feeling that he had abandoned her when she needed him.

And she thought, too, that not smoking was making her crazy.

After a bad three months or so, she was writing again, was "cured."

By now, although she had run out of unemployment compensation some time ago (with considerable relief, actually), Eliza's income had increased; those safe old investments from her dead father's firm, plus some new Xerox urged on her by Smith, had gone up to a point at which, if she exercised great care—few clothes, no trips or expensive wines and *no cigarettes*—she could live on that income without a part-time job. This realization at first made her a little nervous: so much freedom, she was almost guilty about it. But then she decided that the gift of time was wonderful—was possibly deserved? Less sure of that, she was thrifty with those hours, as well as with her money. She worked hard, four or five hours a day. Producing new poems, revising old ones.

And she sold them! Not too often: four one year, six the next, but steadily, so that slowly she began to believe that she was a poet; she was not famous, but she was a published poet.

And that was a source of steady happiness to her, that work, that small success.

With the poems themselves she was not entirely satisfied. (But should a poet be satisfied?) They seemed to her, sometimes, too small and cautious, too "well made." And she had, sometimes, a dizzying sense of other, larger and stronger poems that she could be writing; but perhaps she would. For the most part she was content to work, and to let the direction and the scope of her poetry change as it would.

Then she and Catherine both had sore throats, requiring doctors and drugs. There were plumber's bills, an increased property tax. All in all, she was about seven hundred dollars in debt. Not terrifying (not quite), but too much to owe. She went to a temporary-employment agency and got a job. Since she was a Medical Secretary, and had admitted to literary skills (not mentioning poetry), she was sent to "help out" a psychoanalyst named Dr. Bout, who, in addition to his practice, was writing a "psycho-biography" of Douglas MacArthur. Dr. Bout, a tiny, feisty, pale young man, with an energetic, somewhat truculent manner, a pipe—and two thousand pages of manuscript, which his publisher wanted cut down to seven-fifty.

Eliza would have liked to do the work at home, where she could think about it more peacefully; but no, he wanted her there, installed at a desk in the small room next to his office. She soon understood that he wanted to watch what she was doing, her dangerous activity.

He also wanted her to empty the ashtray, between patients, and to tidy up the magazines in the waiting room.

And he wanted his manuscript magically diminished to the proper length without cutting any words from the original.

She managed to stand two weeks with Dr. Bout. Two hundred dollars.

.   .   .

Four weeks in a Child Guidance Clinic, a much nicer place. Five hundred dollars.

Out of debt, she was more than ever aware of her luck: her small and almost adequate income, her small and perfectly private house.

Her sporadic "love affairs" were more like encounters than affairs, and they occurred at increasing intervals as she devoted less and less time to them. Often they left her lonelier than before. She missed Harry very much.

"I don't know," she said to Kathleen, who continued to call her, although often Eliza felt that their rather accidental friendship was over. Still, she had to say something. "I'm always attracted to men, some men, but it doesn't seem to work out. Maybe I should have married Harry. He's such a terrific friend."

"He would have taken up too much of your time." Kathleen had met Harry once and did not like him; he talked too much, even interrupting her. (Harry did not like Kathleen, either. "She's really in love with you, and that's what makes her so cross—can't you see that, Eliza?")

"How's Miriam?" Eliza asked.

"Well, she spent the weekend in L.A., and I have the weirdest feeling that she got together with Lawry. I don't know why, I'm just sure."

"Kathleen, come on, that's so unlikely—"

"Well, she was up to something down there, I know that."

Not smoking, Eliza was acutely aware of those who did. She had observed that Kathleen's style of smoking was as hostile as her conversation; she blew smoke everywhere, all over everyone, and she scattered ashes about.

How had she herself smoked, Eliza wondered, and she concluded that her own style had been simply greedy, a devouring. Josephine smoked in a discreet and ladylike way, while Daria's smoking was furtive, and ashamed.

Daria was in a sanatorium in New Hampshire, being treated for a depression that had lasted since her last miscarriage. Josephine and Eliza discussed this on the phone: Daria was their subject matter. Smith commuted from Woodside to New Hampshire to see Daria, and to stop by Washington on some sort of business.

"I must say that Smith has been a saint" was one of the things that Josephine often said.

And generally Eliza would murmur some agreement. But on other days she would be disinclined to such ready praise of Smith, and she would say, "He's almost too good about it, don't you think? He's settled too easily into this role, the man with the ailing wife."

"Well, what else could he do?" Brisk, practical Josephine, but an edge had come into her voice.

"Oh, I don't know. I don't mean something specific. It's just a sense I have."

"You've always been awfully hard on Smith—"

"When they got married, you said yourself that there was something about him."

This conversation, which was begun with good will, and true mutual concern about Daria, ended sourly, almost acerbically.

Sometimes Josephine would ask how Eliza's work was going, but that did not turn out well either. She would ask on days when Eliza did not want to talk about it, when it was going terribly—she would never be able to finish a poem again. Or Josephine would forget to mention a poem that Eliza had recently published. "Oh, the *Atlantic?* I was sure you said it would be in *Harper's.*"

This was the worst, the most overt not getting along with Josephine since Eliza's adolescence. Was that an effect of not smoking?

She was also getting along badly with Catherine. Catherine, in her middle teens, passively watching older kids, the hippies. Waiting.

Eliza's conflict with Catherine was cruder and more predictable than with Josephine, and it was *terrible,* frightening to Eliza.

"One o'clock is much too late for a girl of your age to come home. I said *eleven.*"

"Well, the show got out late, and we went—"

"Catherine! I'm not asking you where you went, or why. I'm telling you to come home when I say."

"But next weekend there's this party, at the Fillmore—"

"You're too young for late parties, or the Fillmore."

Feeling the heat of her own face, and the rising pressure of her blood, Eliza had a sudden and horrifying sense of being someone else, of being inhabited by another person. Standing there, her arms unforgivingly akimbo, she felt herself to be not Eliza but Josephine: she *was* Josephine, yelling at herself, Eliza, Catherine.

"How much longer do I have to do what you say?" asked Catherine.

Then, as suddenly as it had come, that Josephine-possession left, and Eliza was herself again, in her own kitchen in the sun, looking at Catherine, who was so very serious and young that she was almost funny. (Had Josephine ever mildly smiled at Eliza, at the end of such a scene? Eliza doubted it.) "Catherine, how can I answer that?" Eliza in her own voice, gently, smiling, asked. "Until you start to work, or get married, or something. Catherine, do you know that you're impossible?"

"I don't want to work, or particularly get married. I don't much like boys. I just want a lot of babies."

"Oh, my God—"

But by now they were feeling better, in the pretty and unusually tidy kitchen, in the April sun.

Pouring coffee for them both, Eliza (still, almost automatically) began to reach for a cigarette. And then did not.

Months later, she recognized that she felt better physically than she ever had; the world smelled and tasted much better; she had more energy. But for years, she was sometimes conscious of a lack, a nameless loss, and sometimes she would dream that she was smoking.

13 / Josephine: Notes Toward an Autobiography

I am too old to be so upset about my daughters: don't children ever stop? Their endless childhoods, and now what seems to me their endless immaturity.

A terrible mistake, two daughters ten years apart. I was too young for Eliza, too old for Daria, and now I feel punished by them both.

I have decided that if I write things down in an orderly way, trying to sort them out, perhaps I will see more clearly. (I very much doubt that I will publish this.)

Eliza: The hateful truth is that Eliza has always been at war with me, and always she has known how to make me most uncomfortable. Is it possible that we are secretly alike? Our lives so far might suggest this: (more hateful truth) we both married at twenty, in both cases because we were pregnant, and both our husbands later committed suicide. "Coincidence" does not seem the right word; it looks more like doom.

I wonder: is it to separate herself from me that Eliza is writing poetry? What she doesn't know is that I was a published poet for a while. Not in magazines that she would consider good; I wrote light verse for the *Post*, sometimes a woman's magazine. It was so easy, so unrewarding that I gave it up. When I contemplate the work of a biography, hours in libraries and museums (my cold feet in the British Museum, pneumonia in Yorkshire: Charlotte Brontë), the correspondence with uncooperative sources—when I think of all that, poetry seems an almost silly exercise, a childish toying with words.

Eliza's poems do not seem to me remarkable.

And I wonder is she writing poetry because it is the literary form I care for least? For which I have really no respect? She should have known some of the poets I have known. Doesn't she remember them coming to our house on Washington Square when she was a little girl? Narcissistic drunks, most of them.

Eliza does not understand political reality: since we are not living in a classless society, there is no point in pretending that we are. I would fight for the rights of all minorities, write articles, send checks, but I would not necessarily invite them to parties in my house; they would not like it there.

Daria: She does not understand about money, any more than Eliza understands social realities. Several hundred thousand dollars just given away before Smith stopped her. She used to weep over every horror story in the news, before Smith stopped her from reading papers, listening to the news. I would have thought that Daria would write poetry, if either of them did, and that Eliza would do something strong, like medicine or law.

Daria and I both were married in the orchard of this house (our two first weddings, that is), and I rather imagine that Daria, should her marriage come apart, would not remarry—unlike Eliza, who married Evan in City Hall, New York.

Weddings: The awful thing, at my wedding to Caleb, in the orchard (aside from being pregnant, bad enough), was—

that morning, the morning of my wedding, I got a note in the mail, forwarded from the *Atlantic,* accepting an article, my first, and I thought, My God, why am I getting married? I could have been a writer—only that—without all these intimacies, these debilitating relationships. These daughters.

But I had to admit to myself: I was pregnant because I had seduced Caleb, much more my fault than his. I was curious, one snowy Thanksgiving when his parents were visiting mine, in this very house. I wondered what it would be like to go on as we were in front of the fire, kissing, "petting," still wearing our outdoor snow clothes. I was the one who said, "It's so hot, all these clothes, shouldn't we take some off? Here, Caleb, you have so many buttons, I'll help." I can still hear my disingenuous girlish voice, and see Caleb, his blond face flushed from the fire, not quite sure what to do, but listening to me, and doing it.

Did Eliza seduce Evan? It seems quite likely to me, such a passive Southern boy, although quite handsome, as her father, Caleb, was.

My second marriage, to Franz, took place in some unremembered office in Maryland, because he thought the idea amusing. "How amusing to marry a blue-eyed Bostonian American in Maryland," he said, in his feeling-hiding way, in his beautiful voice. We did not ever talk about love, and I was almost embarrassed by the feelings he brought to my body, endlessly. How beautiful he made me feel; again, and again, without words.

When Franz was killed—"killed in Spain," "dead in Madrid," how horribly romantic those phrases are—then I wanted to die; that also sounds romantic, but it is true. I was depressed, if that is the word, for more than a year. (What can Daria possibly know about depression?)

Then I met Jason, and he kept saying, "How beautiful you are," which, since I am not beautiful, should have told me something of his character. But instead I imagined that he could somehow repeat Franz for me, not knowing that he would be an exacerbation of my grief. I married him in the orchard, because he wanted to.

He only took up my time, and provided me with a tiny daughter who refused to eat. And all the time there was Eliza, watching us hate each other.

Suicides: It was inexcusable, what Caleb did to me, and I do not believe for a minute that it had to do with the stock market. After all, he killed himself in March, five months after the Crash, when I was four months pregnant. He was angry at me; he hated being married. And none of that was my fault.

But when Evan Quarles killed himself, my first thought, an absolutely inadmissable one, was this: Ah, so now it's happened to you. I was deeply shocked at myself, but later I was able to be kind, and at least I was glad that they had done it in such different ways, Caleb's leap and Evan's pills and bourbon.

Naturally enough, I have sometimes worried about Smith.

Two Acres: Woods, pine and fir, birch, hemlock. In the orchard, grass and apples. Stone fences. The house—granite, oak timbers. The long porch, scraggly lawn, a coarse gray beach. The lake. Water, islands, mountains.

Where I am, what I have.

And, having written down all those personal horrors, I cannot say that I feel particularly better.

I do not think that I will write an autobiography, ever.

14 / Daria and the White House

We are invited to the White House, and the truth is I find it absolutely impossible to go.

I try to tell Smith this. He does not believe me, or he thinks I am merely shy.

I am considering another attempt, a confrontation during which I tell him the truth: I cannot go to the W.H., because if I did I would shoot the President. Would Smith believe that? I doubt it, although it *is true*. Shoot-the-President is a much stronger inner imperative than any of my old money give-away orders.

I have even picked out the gun. It is the smallest in Smith's collection, really tiny. Pretty, even. It will fit into any bag. *(Will?)*

What I feel for the P. is a hatred that goes beyond hating; it is a careful, meticulous loathing. His small dishonest eyes and ugly twisted mouth. I visualize him naked: the dark matted body hair and shriveled sex. Most nakedness is human, vulnerable— Smith's is—but the P.'s is merely hideous.

Smith has already been to the W.H.; he has met the P. and those other people, although not the P.'s family, those plastic women whom I would not even bother to kill. He did not admit it in detail, but Smith was disappointed. He had, of course, seen the man endlessly on television; nevertheless I am sure he expected some personal grandeur that the cameras had somehow missed—the truth being, of course, that they show him at his grandest, made up for spotlights. What I understood from Smith, most of all from his ultra-Bostonian voice, was a tone of disappointed snobbery. Although P., the P. is visibly, irrevocably and undisguisably lower-class. No matter what he wears or where he goes with whom, as Shady Hill—Groton—Harvard—Fly Club, Smith would be the first to recognize. (Christ, the Kennedys were bad enough, those cheap rich Micks: he has never said that, but I have heard it in his voice.)

In any case, now we are invited. Do the guards search everyone? Even "attractive young women" who are married to "promising" (very rich conservative) young men? I see myself in something very retrogressively flounced and flowered, perhaps a castoff of Josephine's; that would be a good joke, but who could I tell? Shy, demure, a little stupid (he'd find that appealing). Until—BANG.

The truth is I probably lack the nerve, or I would probably explode with pure hatred in the presence of the P. But I like to think about killing him.

It would—or it might—be different if I had a terminal disease, if I had *the* disease. But with such small breasts I think the smallest lump would be apparent, and there are none. (Surely this is the truly craziest wish I have ever had, to *wish* for C?) But I hate the idea of dying "mowed down" by Secret Service bullets, and surely that is what would happen. Or maybe I would be jailed and somehow injected with C, like all those people who killed J.F.K.

I may tell Reed Ashford, our new old-family-friend, about this; he might help?

(Smith says that we should invite him to dinner soon with some "appropriate" girl. But I don't know any girls like that. I will invite him with Eliza. It will be a disaster.)

. . .

I am (sadly) not actually going to kill the P.; I only think about it. I am probably going to stay married to Smith, in my own white well-guarded house. But I do not think I will accompany Smith to the White House.

Too dangerous, all around.

And Reed is dangerous. Should I shoot him instead? Then, in that caught moment before the shot, would he notice me more? Now he looks at me as though we were much older friends than we are; there is always a suggestion that eventually we will talk, or something, together.

The P., I am sure, hates fucking. He never fucks. Twice, maybe, those children. But not for fun.

Would a psychiatrist tell me that my wish to shoot the P. is a "sexual" wish? Maybe; I don't think so.

How does Reed feel about sex, fucking? I must find out; I think we feel the same.

If I shoot the P., I will not find out anything. It is only a joke that I think about, sometimes.

15 / Fantastic Sex

"And this is Reed Ashford, whom we met two years ago in Amsterdam," said either Daria or Smith to Eliza, and Eliza, intent on Daria, who was recently declared "well," didn't even try to catch the name. But she registered, as people do, a great deal more than she was conscious of: extreme blond handsomeness, most obviously—a small man, perfectly made. And also a kind of tender gentleness, a desire to please. Some innate loneliness. And a strain of violence, as though he were saying: Come close, and I'll break you apart. (The two faces that Daria saw in Amsterdam.)

However, Eliza was too busy observing Daria to be conscious of those confused reactions to a too attractive young man. Daria, cured, was a young Woodside matron, the wife of a success. And that was how she looked: beautifully dressed, of course, in pleated white silk. Serious rather than sad, and showing at least a perfunctory interest in every conversation, although not initiating any talk herself. She seemed older than she was; her eyes were a little tired, a little glazed.

And Eliza found herself—curiously, half consciously— imitating her sister; she, too, was unaccustomedly proper, and more than a little perfunctory. At some point she asked that over-attractive young man, whose name she had already lost, what he did in Europe; he had referred to a great many trips.

"Oh," he answered, smiling beautifully and vaguely, "I sort of buy things for people."

Not terribly interested—she was only making conversation—Eliza took this to mean that he traveled for fun and liked buying presents for friends, making a sort of occupation out of shopping, as terribly rich women seem to do. Much later she understood that he was a buyer, professionally, for antique and import-export stores, for decorators—anyone. And he was not, in fact, rich; he only had that air.

Daria's husband was plumper and softer with success. Predictably, he had become an expert on wines; more surprising, he was interested in politics. Trips to Washington, for a long time now. A vague air of knowingness.

And Eliza remembered that at some point he and Daria were invited to the White House; they were going, and then did not.

Although she knew that the trip might be dangerous ground—it was still assumed that she and Smith disagreed on everything, that he probably considered her crazy—because she had thought of it, she asked, "You didn't go to Washington, after all?"

Daria giggled in a loud and sudden way, quite out of keeping with her proper clothes, her hostessy demeanor (as Smith alarmedly recognized). "We thought it might be dangerous," Daria said, and she laughed again.

Eliza, however, had liked her sister's laugh; to her it was a glimpse of the old pre-depressed Daria, the lovely, hypersensitive, quick-to-laugh-or-cry girl that Eliza had known all her life. And so, in a superior way, Eliza said to Smith, "Dangerous to national security, I hope?"

Smith reddened, and at the same time looked very sad.

"Well, it certainly could have been interesting," said the beautiful blond man; although he had spoken rather neutrally, Eliza took this as a defense of Smith, and she regarded him with distaste.

Smith spoke into an unfriendly silence: "This is a rather nice Pinot Chardonnay, don't you think? Just dry enough."

The house that Smith found and bought for himself and Daria and for the children that he still envisioned was huge, of course, an enormous fortress of a house, on a thickly wooded hillside. It was literally hidden among the trees, the massive cedars and elms, poplars and eucalyptus. Giant precisely trimmed boxwoods guarded the entrances and lined the paths, and strategically placed spotlights illuminated the shrubbery at night. No one could possibly enter that house, or leave it, unseen.

The dining room was long, low-ceilinged, the table manorial; to Eliza, the setting was as oppressive as the present conversation. White uniformed maids served a succession of predictable dishes: crab salad, overdone lamb with potatoes, something chocolate and too rich.

Looking across at Daria, whose head now drooped, her eyes wavering with fatigue, Eliza quickly imagined that her sister was imprisoned: drugged, restrained. But then she looked at Smith, his brown-eyed, clear-browed American niceness, and she knew that her imaginings were melodrama. She thought of this ability Smith had—always to make her feel crazy. Wrong, and silly: surely writing poetry is a silly thing to do?

Coffee in the living room.

And then the young man, an unlikely source, offered escape. Turning to Eliza, "I don't know about you, but I have an awfully early day tomorrow. Would you care for a ride back to the city?"

And Eliza, who had been planning to stay over, rather

gratefully accepted. No matter that she didn't like him much.

Goodbyes were said, they walked out into the night, the dark.

Seeing his battered car, she even began to like him a little, and she liked him better when he said, "Well, it's always nice to leave a party, don't you think? I've got some pretty good dope. Would you like some? Frankly, I could use it."

By the time they got to her house, they were fairly stoned. Once inside, they fell upon each other. They seized each other, kissing; kissing, they fell onto the sofa, holding, kissing. But because they were so high it was all very gentle, deliberately slow, and into Eliza's foggy mind flashed scenes from her adolescence; she saw, or felt herself, necking with lovely boys, all tender and young, as she was then, on sofas or back seats of cars, in darkness, late at night. Even Evan; even she and Evan had had such moments for a while.

And as gently as they kissed they disengaged; they looked at each other and laughed, and he said, "I've got two more joints—"

"Lovely, and would you care for some wine?"

They laughed again, really breaking up, and Eliza went into the kitchen.

He is younger than me, she thought—and much more blond. A blue-eyed marvel, his face a miraculous balance of planes and lines, he is *very* beautiful. She who had never liked beautiful men, who at first did not like this one, at that moment could not care less.

Coming back with cold wine and glasses on a tray, she asked, "Is that just plain grass, really?"

"Well, I think it's been doctored a little."

Eliza poured wine, and spilled a little—this, too, seemed hilarious. And dizzily she was thinking, Terrific, we'll have a marvelous night in bed; lucky that Catherine's away. I don't like him much, really, but it doesn't matter—we won't talk much, or should I stop these one-night stands? Her mind, as she thought all this, was quite remote—was someone else's mind.

Nothing about this man made sense, least of all her being with him; and nothing mattered except this sexual urgency between them, and a seemingly shared instinct to delay, to postpone its consummation.

He said, "I like your house. Very much. This is lovely wood," and he ran his hand along the tabletop. "Lovely," he said again as his hand caressed the wood, just as her hand had, in the long refinishing process.

Watching him, Eliza was aware of a hot tightening in the bottom of her stomach. "I have a thing about wood," she said tensely.

"Do you? So do I." He smiled.

They had lit the two new joints, and now they began to laugh again, choking a little. And then, there on the sofa, they kissed again.

At last he said, "Look, we really have to go to bed. It's time."

"Yes."

What happened between them in Eliza's wide low bed was an acting out of all sexual fantasies, all at once, all fantasies of making love with everyone, with all differences of gender blotted out, all apertures and extremities in use, all violently, at once.

And even while it was going on Eliza was aware of what was happening, and a part of her mind was thinking that it must be the drug, whatever it was that had been added to the grass. And she observed, too, that nothing that was happening had anything to do with "love"—with "being in love."

In the morning, presumably sober, they made love again, wonderfully.

. . .

Even the day to which they had awakened was amazing: warm and golden, with gentle sunshine lying across the Bay, a light breeze rustling the eucalyptus just outside Eliza's bedroom window, scents of lemon and spice wafting in to where they lay. A romantic smell—a lovely and possibly romantic day. Why, then, did Eliza feel so queasy?

She said, having resolved some time ago to be more straightforward with men, "I feel funny."

"Funny?" He considered. "You're either madly in love or possibly you're hungry. Or it could be both?"

She laughed. He was, then, a nice person. But it came to her that what she felt was a little crazy, in her own familiar room, in her own bed that she had refinished laboriously and lovingly herself. She was somehow disoriented.

Quite seriously, he announced, "There's something I have to tell you."

He was propped up on one elbow, and now he laughed a little at the stagy momentousness of what he had said, and she laughed, too, but her heart sickened suddenly. Was he going to say that he was married, or in love with someone else? Was *she* in love?

He asked, "Tell me, last night when Smith introduced us, did my name mean anything—ring any bell for you?"

Was he a criminal, famous for something terrible? She murmured no while her mind continued its dark imaginings.

"It may not be really important, I don't think it should be," he was saying, "but I was a student at Raleigh—in fact, just before—"

The most beautiful boy in the world. "No, I really don't want to know his name. Why should I?" Eliza had said somewhat angrily to Evan just after his confession. And so "Reed Ashford" had meant nothing at all to her, the night before.

Her queasiness had mounted to her throat; it was lodged there, stuck.

Now Reed was saying that of course he knew Mr. Quarles was not gay ("gay"—Christ! what a word for poor Evan), but there was something funny; he used to see him everywhere. Eliza then had a wrenching vision of Evan following a boy around, not knowing what to do. ("It's enough to make me wonder if I could be queer.")

Eliza wondered if she had felt strange, queasy before because of the imminence of this revelation—of its aura, so to speak? In any case, she felt much stranger now; she was both incredulous and aware of a kind of horrible logic in all this. Just as she was thinking, Why me, she also thought, Of course it would be me. Of course *inexorably*, this word clangs in her mind, of course he and Daria and Smith would meet in Amsterdam, and they would bring him home to me.

Reed said, "I started to mention it to Daria and Smith in Amsterdam when they said your name, Eliza Quarles, but I wasn't sure, and Daria seemed so delicate—I might have upset—"

Inexorably, this had to happen, Eliza thought. And she thought of the other violent coincidences in her life: a suicided father and husband, too.

"Lovely Eliza," Reed said, and he stroked her bare arm. "I'm sorry if I've upset you. But, you see, I thought I should say it. Eventually something about Raleigh would have come up."

Then they are to see each other again? This was not another one-night stand? Of course it was not; and, recognizing this, Eliza felt, all at once, ill and elated, warmly glad and helplessly trapped.

"Suppose I make breakfast? I'm good at that." He was smiling in the clear, cleansed way of one who has confessed.

Looking at him, Eliza thought, Of course, he knew perfectly well that Evan had fallen in love with him. He might even have encouraged Evan, in his way.

He walked out of the room, and Eliza was left with an

agony for Evan such as she had not felt for years—had not felt since his death. An agony and a new sickness of her own; she had not before been so much and so sickly "in love." (Surely that was what was the matter, really?) Her very surroundings were strange and unfamiliar, her own bedroom, familiar books and pictures were alien.

And now "the most beautiful boy in the world," Reed Ashford, came into her bedroom with a tray: her white wicker tray, full of breakfast. He had found everything, including the tray; he had made bacon and toast and eggs, poured juice, while she was still lying there, trying to digest the fact of who he was, to digest her own tangled and tattered feelings.

Perhaps because she was still preoccupied with that, with what still seemed both fated and a wild coincidence, Eliza recognized but did not consciously think of another important quality in Reed: he was a man used to taking care of women; he chose that role, even with Eliza, who was certainly not used to being taken care of by men. By way of thanking him, but laughing a little, she said, "You're really incredible."

"But you're still bothered, aren't you," he said to her as they ate. "About Mr. Quarles. Its turning out to be me." Intuitiveness was perhaps Reed's most striking quality—or, possibly, he was no more intuitive than other people were, but he listened, was wholly attuned to his intuitions.

Eliza said, "Yes. I am."

"Well, why not treat it as the kind of ordinary coincidence that really happens all the time? People turning out to know other people. You know, especially people who go to a certain group of schools during certain years. Try thinking on that level."

Speaking so sensibly (if very slightly unconvincingly), Reed had left out the reason for his pursuit of the connection with Daria and Smith, despite his boredom and annoyance with Smith—which was his strong attraction to Daria. He had recognized her as his *type;* she was so familiar to him. She was as familiar as the woman whom he was, in fact, to see that afternoon, his married love of several years.

But Eliza smiled at what sounded sensible, and smiled her agreement and her thanks.

Outside, the day was clearer and brighter and warmer, moving toward noon. The beginning of summer as it might be in a place with less aberrant weather than San Francisco has.

Reed said, "I have to go now, but tonight—what time can I see you? How early? We'll go out, okay?"

He left, and Eliza got out of bed, but she was halted by the small problem of what to wear. It was not simply the rare warm weather that had created a problem; after all, she had some cotton clothes. It was rather that she was not sure, that day, how to dress—who to be. She would go downtown, she thought; would perhaps buy something to wear tonight, but as what person would she go downtown, in what persona? As an upper-middle-class white woman in her thirties (Miriam's friend), or as a young poet "in love"? And what could she possibly buy, what could she wear with Reed Ashford? For the moment, she settled on an old cotton dress in which she would be comfortable, if not invisible, which was what (and *why?*) she had at last understood that she would like to be today.

The weather had affected everyone. Tourists babbled crazily, snapping pictures of each other, on and off the cable cars, screeching over hills. People in wild gaudy clothes crashed cymbals, shook tambourines and danced—at nearly noon, in the middle of Union Square.

Eliza wandered in and out of familiar stores, aimless, looking. It was as though she were in a foreign city. It was even surprising when she approached clusters of people and realized that they were speaking English. A sudden smell reminded her of Rome; she smiled as she saw that it came from a bus's exhaust fumes.

In I. Magnin, at a distance, she saw Gilbert Branner, who was leafing through expensive ties (of course), who did not see her. In Macy's, at a lesser distance, there was The Lawyer, looking at socks, also not seeing her. Perhaps she really was invisible? She wished strongly that she would see Miriam; Miriam would see her. Instead, on Grant Avenue, arm in arm, there were Peggy and Ted Kennerlie, who saw her, and greeted her with an enthusiasm that she recognized as entirely false.

"Eliza, how are you? You look marvelous, so cool in that dress. What do you hear from Harry?"

"Who?" With a shock she realized that she had for the moment almost forgotten who Harry was: Harry her favorite friend-lover. "Not much, for a while," she said.

She was not dressed up enough to be talking to the Kennerlies. She got this clear message from Ted—and especially not on lower Grant Avenue, in fact right in front of Saks. And so with a perfunctory smile she slipped into the store, as they headed toward Doro's, to celebrate something, whatever. In Saks, Eliza did not buy a new dress, or anything.

Coming out of Saks, after her short restless tour of the store, she glanced into the traffic, then at its noontime heaviest, and for an instant her heart stopped: scowling but beautiful, looking dead ahead, there was Reed Ashford, in his unmistakable Plymouth. It would be so easy to slip out between the stopped cars, even to wave and shout to him. Why, then, did she not? Why did she, in fact, sink backward, out of his possible sight?

She was dizzy, suddenly, with the heat, with fatigue and incomprehension; too much was getting through to her, and none of it was making sense.

She took a bus home.

Two black women were seated across the aisle from her, talking in a loud and comfortable way to each other, old friends. The one who was talking more was saying, "All things I've ate all my life, now I can't eat any more. Now they make my stomach cramp up. Onions. Turnips." She was a big woman, with some dark down on her upper lip; she and Eliza did not look at all alike, but Eliza had a compelling sense that she *was* that woman; she was watching and listening to herself. When the woman got off the bus, she smiled protectively in Eliza's direction. But why? Why this friendly sense of slipping back and forth, of being other people? Why was she sometimes invisible?

Reed came somewhat later than he said he would, and Eliza, who had been almost faint with longing, with anxiety (faint from whatever cause) fell upon him with kisses, as he did her, with love. They endlessly kissed, murmuring love to each other.

Later they smoked more joints, and drank some wine.

At some hour of the night or early morning, they went down to the kitchen and made eggs, mounds of eggs. Coffee, toast. They were too dazed and tired to talk, to do anything but laugh a little, lightly, and then to sigh with love.

Most of their nights were like that, over the summer.

"A love affair that is empty at the center, a world with no central flame. Dirt flying apart," Eliza wrote in her notebook. She doubted that a poem would come of that, and she believed that she was in fact flying apart, was out of control.

Often after Reed had made love to her, she dreamed of flowers: once a branch of almond blossoms, flowering, sweetly scented; and on another night an alpine New England meadow, a Maine meadow of wildflowers, of all colors. The triteness of this made her smile; nevertheless, those were her dreams.

Reed lived in what was a shack, on Stinson Beach—a shack that very few people had ever seen. Eliza had not. "Darling, it's terribly cold and foggy there most of the summer. We'll go for a weekend in the fall, when it's nice. Besides, I love your house. It seems made for us. Perfect," he had said to her.

The young married woman with whom he had been involved—Rosalyn, who looked so much like Daria—was one of the few people who had ever been there, and that had happened at a time when Reed was short of money, really short; and two or more afternoons a week in motels were too much for him. Perversely, Rosalyn, who was extremely rich, loved it there: the small drafty rooms, the sagging furniture and irremediable smell of must were to her exotic, and aphrodisiac in a way that no posh motel could ever be.

That summer Rosalyn was at Tahoe with her husband and children—happily for Reed, who was wildly in love with Eliza. But Rosalyn phoned a lot, and she had begun to understand that Reed was infrequently at home, no matter when she called. Clever, up to a point, in her own way, instead of accusing him she spoke sadly and tenderly. "Darling, I miss you so badly; nothing is beautiful without you. Sometimes I cry." This worked; she had some insight into Reed. It worked to the extent that he was prevented from saying, It's over between us, I love someone else; someone marvelous, someone I *really* love. He sometimes thought that he would say that, but not now, not when she was crying over his lack.

He felt rather kindly toward Rosalyn, who was very beautiful, more beautiful, really, than Daria was—with whom he had enjoyed many long afternoons of love.

Then Rosalyn began to urge Reed to come up to Tahoe. Her husband traveled back and forth, went everywhere on business. "Darling, it would be so easy. Darling, I can't wait. It's been so long."

Reed made excuses, almost hoping that they were transparent.

He was getting low on money. He was "between trips," as he put it to himself. He liked to arrange his business life so that profits from one trip would pay for the purchases on the next, which entailed going back to Europe almost as soon as his cargoes had arrived, been sold and paid for. He had waited too long; his last antiques—the silver and brass and pewter, from Verona—arrived and were sold in May. Now, in early August, midstream in his summer of great love, he was running low; he would have to scurry around for advance money for his next trip, which was what he most hated to do. Having grown up in Hollywood, he was used to financial extremes—the son of a sometimes-rich-and-famous movie star, and an equally erratic director. Still, he hated the bottom areas, the lowering, the necessary scrounging.

Of course he told Eliza none of this, any more than he would mention Rosalyn to her.

Eliza was concerned with Catherine's impending return; the entrance of reality into their life, as she thought of it. What, strangely, did not concern her was the fact that she had done no writing at all over the summer. A few scribbled notes, lines here and there that could be called sketches for a portrait, a portrait not necessarily of a person. Perhaps simply of a state of mind—a summer.

But no poems. She thought of this without worrying about it. She believed that once the summer was over everything would settle down. Poems would surface almost automatically.

Out with Reed in a restaurant, Eliza, although "madly in love," was not entirely at ease. She was a pretty woman, she knew that, who probably looked five or six years younger than she was, and Reed was only five years younger than she. And why should that matter, which person was older? Perhaps it didn't. What did matter, and she was sure of this, was his most conspicuous, compelling beauty. Women and men, too, stared at him as though dazzled by the sun. And so Eliza, after all those years, was given a late and terribly pained insight into poor

Evan; she could see (she could even feel herself to *be*) poor doomed Evan, dazzled, following Reed about, not knowing at all what to do with what he felt. (Sometimes she felt the same.)

They did not talk about Evan. Reed hardly knew him, after all, and Eliza had nothing to say. Certainly she couldn't talk about her sense of *being* Evan, and in an idle way she wondered if this love affair would end by killing her. Was that why she had met Reed?

Catherine was to come back on a certain day late in August, and so Eliza and Reed decided that he would stay away, in Stinson, for a few days after that. It would be a chance for Eliza and Catherine to see each other and (Reed did not say this) a chance for him to pull his affairs together.

Nothing went according to their plan.

Just as Reed, at Stinson Beach, was sadly distributing some of his effects from the overnight bag that since early summer had been at Eliza's house, he heard from outside the high whine of a familiar engine (like most Californians, he was sensitive to cars); he heard the slam of a known door, and there was Rosalyn's brown Jag, and Rosalyn, herself quite brown, and thin and lithe, in crisp sheer white.

He went to the door. They embraced. She was lovely, and there were tears in her gray-green-yellow eyes. How could Reed not be glad to see her?

He was glad, but what she wanted (this was instantly clear) was to make love right away—to reseal, as it were, their being in love. And Reed was not ready for that.

He disengaged himself from her sharp and demanding embrace, and said, "Let me get you a drink."

Rosalyn smiled mistily. "Okay, but don't be long."

When he came back, with tall, postponing gin-and-tonics (her favorite), Rosalyn was stretched out on his lumpy studio couch, her shirt unbuttoned to white net, brown breasts.

He sat beside her, reflecting on the oppositeness of Rosalyn and Eliza: Eliza's body was generous and warm, voluptuously soft, whereas Rosalyn's was smooth and cool, spare, firm. He suddenly thought how fantastic it would be to be in bed with both of them. (He had never done this, or seriously thought of it before.) To be made love to simultaneously by two such separately beautiful girls.

In the meantime, Rosalyn unbuttoned his shirt, then reached for the buckle of his belt, and Reed thought, Well, why not? Why not let Rosalyn make love to me?

He did. He was excited by her mouth, her tongue, her fingers probing him. Lying almost still, Reed savored long delicious moments of her caressing.

But he had forgotten Rosalyn, really forgotten her, and she was in her way as spoiled, as in love with herself, as he was. She suddenly, shrilly cried out, "Christ, Reed, you're so passive! I might as well be screwing a dildo!" In an awful, unfamiliar voice.

So Reed consummated their act, in a conventional and not very satisfactory way.

Five minutes later, the phone rang. Since he had told a prospective backer—and this must be she—that he would be at home all afternoon awaiting her call, he couldn't not answer.

But it was Eliza. Catherine had come and gone—gone up to Mendocino for a couple of days with some friends she had met over the summer. Catherine was fine, fat but beautiful. Eliza and Reed wouldn't have to spend the night apart. Then she said, "You sound very strange."

"I do? I didn't mean to. That is terrific. I'll see you about seven."

Rosalyn said, "You sounded awfully strange."

"I did? That was a possible business partner. I guess I really don't like the idea."

"A woman? Reed, come on, how much am I supposed to swallow?" Rosalyn was again speaking in her alien, harsh voice.

The possible backer was a woman, an antiques dealer, but Reed felt himself in no position to insist on this. Also, he knew himself to be a poor liar; he did better at confessionals.

"You must be having a really successful summer, business-wise. Spending all your time at it, right?" Unskilled in irony (does any impassioned person do it well?), Rosalyn heard her voice crack; it broke unattractively, which was too much for her pride, for her totally attractive self-image, and she felt that it was Reed's fault—Reed was making her be like this (and of course she was quite right).

Pulling her clothes together, seizing her bag, she got up and went into the bathroom, from which five minutes later she emerged with cool and perfect eyes, smooth mouth and smoothed-out voice.

She extended a thin brown hand to Reed, but then it all came apart, all her plans: tears rushed into her eyes, and she screamed, "You rotten fucking bastard!" She ran out to her car, running knock-kneed, like a furious and awkward child.

Reed hated scenes—his mother had thrived on them. Now, sickly shaken, he went in to take a shower. He felt that he had been infected with germs, but that those germs could possibly be washed away.

Eliza, at a little after seven, greeted him, "Oh, darling, what a *relief!* When Catherine said she was going on to Mendocino, I realized how much I'd dreaded the end of summer, our time together. So tonight seems a marvelous reprieve, a gift. And I made a lovely crab casserole. It won't matter when we eat it." All this was said interspersed with kisses, with strong embraces, increasing in intensity, until the words about the casserole that could be eaten at any time informed Reed that she wanted to make love *then,* right away (as they had often done, near her front door).

Reed did not want to make love. Very gently, he made a slight gesture of withdrawal.

Which Eliza, who was genuinely aroused—for whatever curious reasons—chose to ignore. She kissed him more insistently, touched explicitly.

Reed, more explicitly, withdrew.

And then knowledge, or a vision, exploded like a flash fire in Eliza's mind, and she thought, or *knew,* that he had been with someone else that afternoon. With someone when she called. She could even see him pumping into someone else. (Someone dark and thin, in white: she knew or had intuited his true sexual type, and knew it to be not herself.)

In a voice that was not her own, she said, "You sounded so strange when I phoned."

In fact, she had used Rosalyn's taut, angry voice. Horrified, and dumfounded, Reed explained, lying exactly as he had to Rosalyn. "Yes, a business thing. I haven't told you this, but I've been looking for a sort of backer. She was there."

"That isn't true." By now they were standing and facing each other like enemies, in the hall where they had so often languishingly embraced. And outside was the heavy, invading fog that had so often over the summer enclosed their house, their love.

"You know that isn't true," Eliza repeated in Rosalyn's voice—so that Reed had a sense of being a carrier of some kind of plague; he had infected these two women so that they had become not themselves; they had become interchangeable, and horrible, two harpies.

Helplessly he admitted, "You're right, I was with someone else."

They both understood the sense in which he had meant "was with," but still, if dimly, Reed hoped that the truth would work, would free Eliza from being Rosalyn, that they could talk and be in love again.

This was not what happened. Eliza screamed, "You bastard!" and pushed him toward the door, toward the cold and threatening end-of-summer night.

16 / Detritus:
After Reed

Harry's motel room was so wildly flamboyant as to caricature interior design; someone must have been kidding.

The carpet, so thick that it squished beneath bare feet, was a swirl of greens and purples, a pattern and combination of colors that was repeated in the draperies, with the addition of gold threads, and in the bedspread (heedlessly crumpled on the floor). The lamp bases inexplicably were white, but swirly, too, massively so; more predictably, the shades were parrot-green. In huge gilt frames, on canvas, gigantic flowers echoed the color scheme.

The room's proportions were outrageous, too; it must have been at least a Presidential suite. In fact, the Beatles had once stayed there, or some of them had. And the bed was impossibly vast, was orgiastic in its suggestion.

All in all, it was enough to make anyone laugh, anyone except Eliza, who was lying across the bed with Harry (they were both naked), and she was crying: violently, ragingly, the rage at least in part against the fact of crying. Harry, who was gentle (and at that moment more than a little frustrated), was stroking her shoulder, very slowly.

When she could speak, what Eliza choked out was "That cock-sucking mother-fucking bastard—*goddam* him, what he's done to me!"

What had just happened was that midway in the act of love, when Eliza began strongly to respond, something (perhaps the response itself) reminded her of Reed, of his loss and what she still thought of as his betrayal, and uncontrollably she began to cry. And then to curse.

Sententiously, perhaps, but quite forgivably, Harry said, "Sometimes it's easier to be with someone else when you're happily involved. Not when you're missing someone. Once I had an affair with a married woman who would never see me when her husband was out of town. That struck her as unfair, a betrayal—"

But although well meant, this was exactly the wrong thing to say: he could be describing the behavior of Reed, who while happily involved with Eliza went to bed with someone else. And so she began to cry again.

Harry (newly divorced: the Corsican didn't last long) had just brought out a new movie, a sad grim "realistic" story about adolescents in the desert towns of southern California; they were to see it previewed that night, in San Jose. He listened patiently to Eliza for a while; he patted her shoulder and pulled up sheets and a light blanket, comfortingly. And then he said, softly and sensibly, "Why don't you talk, instead of crying? I think in the long run it'll do you a lot more good."

So, after a few minutes, Eliza did begin to talk. "It doesn't make *sense*, my feeling so terrible about Reed. But I have this terrible pain where I think my heart is. Curious: once I missed someone else very badly, The Consul—and my stomach hurt. It's as though he'd cut something out of me; there's this dreadful lack. Harry, I didn't like him all that much! I like you much more, you know that."

"Sure, baby." He kissed her forehead lightly, lay back down. "We like each other for good, but I have a curious instinct." (Eliza looked over at him, in the bright unreal midafternoon sunlight that escaped through a gap in the draperies; as Harry looked off into some inner space, with those violently pale blue eyes.) "I think more was going on between you and Reed than you understood. I don't think it was just a summer romance, as we used to say. There was a reason for Reed in your life."

"And I can't write any more."

"Well, maybe now you can? Even better? 'Mad Ireland hurt you into poetry.' "

"What?" She half sat up to look at him.

"Mr. Auden on Mr. Yeats."

"Harry, you always surprise me. But I think you're making another romantic movie. Well, I'm sure Reed would be available."

Harry laughed at her. "You're wrong, but it's not a bad idea. In fact, why don't you try to think of it as a movie, or a story? For example, would it help to cast Reed as the dumb blond?"

Finally Eliza laughed, too. She said, "Harry, what in the world would I do without you?"

And some sort of circle seemed to have been completed: having gone from failed sex to anguished tears, to rage, to laughing—they returned to sex. In a slow and most friendly way they made love.

Later, with time to spare between dinner and the movie, they went down to the swimming pool—or, rather, to an area containing several swimming pools. And bright striped deck chairs and plastic lounges and palm trees. And people: old fat people in his-and-hers brilliant Hawaiian outfits. His shirt, her muumuu—too sad and terrible to be anywhere near funny, or so Eliza saw it.

Uncomfortably they chose the least populated pool; swimming up to each other, they almost simultaneously said, "Why do we never go back to Mexico?" (Ixtapanejo: they had never been back.)

"San Jose," lamented Eliza. "Whatever are we doing here?"

"It's a great movie-tryout town. It has the most movie houses per capita, or something."

Harry's movie was superb—Eliza realized later as it replayed in her mind. For the moment, unhappily and uncontrollably, she had reverted to missing Reed, to his vivid lack. In the darkened, smoky theatre, as Harry craned his long neck about, seeking audience reactions, Eliza listened to the Thirties' music (Harry's favorites) from the jukebox, on the sound track. "Body and Soul," "It Had to Be You"—and although Lena Horne, not Billie Holiday (thank God), was singing them, Eliza was thinking, Reed, good Christ, come back, if only for an hour or so.

"Well, how did you like it? Go all right, do you think?" asked Harry.

"Marvelous." She wept.

Rationally, on principle, Eliza did not believe infidelity to be all that bad. She was thinking of this some days later, as alone in her house she waited for Catherine, after another of Catherine's increasing absences. One could do worse things to people than be unfaithful to them, Eliza thought. Reed, on a certain afternoon, with another, unknown woman, performed a certain—"a certain act"? At that phrase her mind stammered, and shuddered to a dead halt. It was *unthinkable*, literally so. She was shivering, as though she had been thrown into a chilly pool, a lake. But nevertheless she made an effort at reason. Well, then, should he have lied? Is that what she was now asking him to have done? Yes. No.

Her blood ran giddily along her veins, and something was pressing down on and enclosing her brain. Her heart hurt, and later, when she could think, she thought that jealousy was as mysterious and as impossible as sex.

Catherine, returned and seated on one of the kitchen's two comfortable chairs, was fat and fair, her hair bleached, skin

browned, blue eyes seemingly bluer from a summer of whatever she had been doing: hiking and camping on Mount Tam-
alpais and up in Mendocino, swimming—watching dawns and
sunsets from high distant places. These were the things she
had been talking about, and, in a fond, bright liberal-mother
way, Eliza had added: Making love, of course she's making
love. She's eighteen, probably been doing it for several years
by now.

Idly, Catherine asked, "What about that guy you were sort
of seeing? The gorgeous little blond one."

Trying to match her diffidence, "I sort of stopped seeing
him," Eliza said. And for an instant she wildly wanted to ask
Catherine: How do you feel about sexual jealousy? Is it really
okay, among you kids, for people to screw anyone at all? Do you
tell each other about it?

But she couldn't ask Catherine this and, recognizing her
own inhibition, Eliza thought, God, I'm as rigid in my way as
Josephine is.

"The pill?" Catherine was asking.

"Darling, I'm sorry. My mind went somewhere else. You
were saying about the pill?" Catherine had started taking the pill
a couple of years ago, mainly (or ostensibly) for irregularities in
her periods.

"Well," Catherine said earnestly, "it never did seem right
to me, when I thought about it. The idea of interfering, I didn't
like it."

"Mm." Eliza absently agreed.

"I don't really like any pills. I must be sort of like you. I've
heard you say, 'I have to be practically dying before I'll take an
aspirin.' "

Catherine with her unaccented California voice had perfectly imitated Eliza's still most–New England accents, of which
she herself was usually not aware. This was a thing that
Catherine had not done before (at least in Eliza's hearing: the
possibilities were frightening). But it was as funny as it was
alarming.

Eliza was still laughing, amusement having triumphed, when she understood that Catherine had continued, in a logical way: Catherine had not been taking the pill, and this summer she met this really neat guy (she even said, "really beautiful") although he had moved on to Hawaii. Had she just now said that she was pregnant? Not exactly: what she said was "And so I'll have the baby in April—isn't that neat?"

Eliza, who had been consciously ready for sexual activity, and half-consciously braced for possible pregnancy, for abortion, now understood with dizzying suddenness that a baby, Catherine's baby, was more than she could contemplate, or sanely imagine.

"Catherine, good God, you're out of your mind," she said weakly, hearing the Bostonian echoes of her own voice (and hearing also Josephine).

"Well, Mom, it's not all that bad. I know your generation is hung up on abortions" (as Eliza thought, We *are?*) "and of course I think if you want one you should get it. But if it's *you,* someone growing inside you, and you really like the father and all, then it's really icky."

"Catherine, you don't understand."

Sweet Catherine continued with the platitudes of her generation as, silently and uncontrollably, Eliza did with those of hers. Or so she later supposed. For the moment, she imagined that blood was rushing around, behind her ears; she couldn't hear anything, couldn't hear what Catherine was saying, or her own unspoken answers.

Earlier, they had been drinking mugs of soup, their favorite lemon-chicken-yoghurt. Eliza now looked down at the pallid swirls of liquid, at the earthenware handle that she still was grasping, and that, with an effort, she did not crash down to the floor.

As Catherine continued to talk about a farm near Mendocino. Cows. A small vegetarian restaurant.

Christ.

. . .

"Well," said Kathleen, over the phone, having listened to Eliza's recital (about Catherine; Eliza had not mentioned Reed), "Catherine has never been exactly an intellectual, would you say? What did you think she'd grow up to do?"

"Oh, I guess get married. Have a lot of children. That's always been in the cards. But, Kathleen, that's what's so terrible; I'm behaving like Josephine. I'm reacting in ways that I don't believe in."

"Well, I've met a lot worse people than your mother. She's really terrific—you never can see that. You should have met mine; she could fill in for Phyllis Diller."

While Kathleen went on about her mother, since whose death she had substituted rage for mourning, Eliza thought of what she herself had just said about reacting in ways that she did not believe in, against her principles. And, speaking of Catherine, she saw that she had been half-consciously talking about Reed, and once more she cursed him for so persisting in her mind.

"I don't much like the idea of abortions either," continued Kathleen. "God help me if I ever have to perform them; in fact, with my mother's help I'm sure He would strike me dead, like He was supposed to do when I left the Church."

Eliza laughed. She said, "That's absolutely great about med school." Kathleen's mother had left her some money; she was applying to medical schools.

"Well, it will be if I get in."

"I know I'm being unfair," Eliza said. "Of course the idea of persuading anyone to have an abortion is monstrous."

"It sure is."

Their conversation was more nearly a joined monologue than a dialogue. Or sometimes they were simply Kathleen's monologues. It was always Kathleen who called, and Eliza who continued to wonder why she did.

"You're not going to believe this," said Kathleen, in the tone of one not caring who believed her, "but guess who's suddenly a star? and rich as all hell."

"A star?"

"*Lawry*, that's who. He finally cut a record, and it's this fabulous success. If you read *Rolling Stone*—or *any*thing—you'd know."

"Well, I guess that's nice."

"*Nice*, Christ, it's a fucking crime against taste. He plays the guitar about as well as I do ballet routines. Nice—Jesus. Anyway, did I tell you Miriam had quit?"

"No, where is she?"

"How in hell should I know?"

Eliza got off the phone as soon after that as she could. She dialed Miriam's number, but no one answered.

During all that warm and lovely fall, the nights continued to be as cold, as fogbound and wind-lashed as at the height of summer. One night, when she was unable to stand anything that was happening, anything in her mind, Eliza did what she had thought of almost daily, and had not done before: she telephoned to Reed in Stinson Beach.

How can one tell when a phone is ringing in an empty house? Eliza could; the insistent tinny sound echoed through those small sea-smelling drafty rooms, where she had never been. He was not there.

That night she slept badly, to be awakened at what seemed a raw, ungodly, early hour: her doorbell. It would have to be Reed, whom she had somehow summoned?

It was not Reed. It was two panting, cross men from Air Express, who had brought her a large and curiously crated box. "All the way up them stairs. Lucky we didn't drop the flithering thing, or break our necks."

This came from the older, heavier man of the two, at whose word "flithering," which she liked very much, Eliza looked up and smiled. He smiled back, a raunchy pirate's grin, and he handed her something to sign. Should she ask him in? What would he make of that? And why not, really? But of course she did not.

Uncrating the box required all Eliza's meager supply of tools; she worked at it until her kitchen was littered with split slats and twisted nails and excelsior, at which some visiting cats sniffed interestedly: another nice present for them.

What it turned out to be was the most ornately and intricately carved small bench (it could be called a footstool) that Eliza had ever seen, or could imagine. To which was attached an envelope with her name, in Harry's familiar bold crazy hand. Inside was a round-trip ticket to Portland, Maine, and a tiny note: "Shouldn't one of these cures work? Love, H."

Harry was somewhere in Texas, shooting.

A week or so later, Eliza and Josephine were in Maine, sitting on those old wicker chairs, on the long porch of that house. September, and Eliza thought how totally unlike a California fall this was. September and sometimes October around San Francisco were hot and yellow, a blur of tawny fading hills, smooth Bay water and golden haze above a pastel city. Whereas in Maine everything was sharpened: colors, shapes of mountains, the very air, which was brilliantly blue and cool. The lake, a deeper blue, was whipped into waves, white-capped with foam, as high as waves in some small foreign sea. Birch leaves fluttered yellow, in clumps near the beach, on the dark green lawn. Behind the house, in the orchard and then the woods, were wildflowers of the most intense purple, most vivid pink or gold. And violent crimson leaves.

Eliza, who had been looking out at the lake, the islands and mountains beyond, now looked down at her hands, which were in even worse shape than usual: nails broken and stained, fingers also stained, and blistered. She had been unable to resist several hours of work on Harry's present; blessing him, she had labored with Jasco and steel wool, sandpaper and most of her muscles.

So far, it had been one of their better visits, for Eliza and Josephine. Josephine had been sympathetic but sensible about Catherine; she had said, in effect, that it was not what they would choose to happen, but what could they do, besides providing some support? And they had also agreed (not surprisingly, given both their histories) that Catherine's decision was probably better than the ones they both made at an age not much beyond hers; it was certainly better not to base a marriage on an unplanned pregnancy. They had agreed, too, that for the moment Daria might well not be told; her history of miscarriages made this delicate.

From Daria they proceeded to Smith, about whom they were more and more able to feel in accord. "God knows how much money he's given those people in Washington," said Josephine, and Eliza muttered agreement.

Most recently, Smith had started a collection of guns. "He seems to forget that I'm the crazy one," Daria had written. "Or that those with guns are often the ones who get shot."

The tone of this had reassured both Josephine and Eliza; they recognized Daria's flashes of wry black wit; when she sounded like that, she was okay, they said to each other.

"It's interesting," mused Eliza. "Daria seems calmer as Smith gets more excited."

"Actually I hope not. I've seen those seesaw marriages. Jason and I were a little like that," said Josephine. (Jason, that Greek shit.)

"Yes, and I hope she doesn't get too calm," agreed Eliza, who then voiced what they both felt: "If only she could be having a child instead of my dumb brainwashed daughter."

"Yes, or if only Smith would let her adopt one."

"Yes, but of course he won't."

"Of course not."

. . .

That night after dinner they decided that it was cold enough for a fire; together they piled up paper, kindling, some birch logs. They lit it and sat back to watch the flames.

"Don't you want some music?" asked Josephine. "I miss the records you girls were always playing. They're all still here. Who was that woman, your favorite?"

"Billie Holiday." But Eliza was not in a mood for hearing Billie. Consciously, she had "got over" Reed, but Billie's voice might reach depths or crevices that she didn't know about, and she wouldn't risk that, not just now. "On the other hand, why not a little Brahms?" she asked, knowing Brahms to be a great love of Josephine's.

Later, as warm violin and piano notes filled the room's empty spaces, Josephine said, "Do you know, I'd never really heard Brahms until I met Franz? Just the trite familiar things."

Eliza knew this, Josephine had said it before; but she knew, too, how passionately Josephine had cared for Franz. Her rare remarks about him arrived like presents.

"I seem to have only minor love affairs," Eliza now said to her mother, possibly by way of exchange. "I had a really foolish one this summer. With a dumb blond."

"Well, possibly that's better for your work? To keep them minor?"

"Possibly." And Eliza laughed, feeling freed, at last, of something.

Almost abruptly, before any of the familiar troubles between them could erupt—and simultaneously—Josephine and Eliza got up to go to bed. "Tired," they both said, and they smiled and bent toward each other, brushing cheeks. Good night.

It was a good night.

Later, in her room, at her desk, in the apple-smelling cool September night, something amazing happened to Eliza. An entire poem arrived, whole, in her mind, so that she had only to write it down, quite quickly.

17 / Daria, Visited by Catherine

Catherine, pregnant and no longer herself a child at all, looks most strange in my gleaming white-on-white living room. She is on her way to Big Sur, in her Levis and bulky red sweat shirt, her hair long and loose, her big chunky dirty feet in sandals.

"Catherine, don't your feet get cold?" I can't help asking, although with Catherine I am not generally maternal.

"Oh, no." She laughs in her fat and placid, tolerant way. "They're used to it."

This is winter, an especially cold January, but Catherine has become a total Californian; she has lost that so identifiable accent which marks the rest of us in our family, and along with it has banished any sense of seasons. She has a Californian's mild surprise at any change in weather; in their blood it is always summer. All year round she is sun-browned, her blond hair is bleached in streaks, her eyes are wide and blue and a little vacant. "Non-intellectual" is what both Josephine and Eliza say about Catherine; the truth is that she is not remarkably bright—"high average" probably, which to either Josephine or Eliza would be dumb. I don't care at all about those things; how could I?

And perhaps since I am so curiously placed in terms of age—ten years younger than Eliza, the exact same number older than Catherine—I am able to like Catherine in a comfortable, non-intimate and thus non-demanding way; which would be impossible for her mother, or, for that matter, for her most demanding grandmother, for Josephine.

I ask her how she feels. Politely, not out of any genuine curiosity, not yet.

"Oh, really neat. He kicks a lot. It feels good."

I wouldn't like that; it's just as well that it didn't happen to me, I think. "You're sure it's a boy?" I ask Catherine.

"Oh, really sure. I can feel it, his being a boy."

"What will he look like?" I am becoming more interested.

Catherine laughs. "Oh, just like his father, I guess. Isn't that how it is with women in our family? What does Josephine always say about it?"

" 'No generic effect' is what she says."

"Well, yes, isn't that true? Mom looks like her father, she says, and she says I look like Evan Quarles, my dad, and you—"

I laugh. "I look like that Greek shit, my old man. But how about that boy, the father of the baby?"

"Oh, he's beautiful, *really*. The most gorgeous blue-black hair, and terrific dark brown eyes, and this fantastic body."

"You don't miss him? You're not sorry he's in Hawaii?"

"Oh, no, he had his thing to do. I know some other people almost as neat. We're friends—I'll let him know about the baby when it's born. He might want to see him, I guess."

"Which island did he go to?"

"Kauai. He says it's really neat there. Flowers and all. Fantastic surf. He's the greatest surfer on the coast."

It is during this conversation that I realize that eventually, somehow, I will be the one to get Catherine's child. Not as my own; she would never give it to me, not stubborn Catherine (nor would Smith ever allow me to adopt a child). But I am sure that it will occur to everyone as a good idea, and in an interested way I will watch to see how this comes about.

· · ·

Smith says, "But you've never wanted to go to Hawaii. I've suggested it."

"Well, now I really do." There are many advantages to being considered a little crazy; and Smith likes having a whimsical wife, whimsy being somehow very wifely.

Thinking about it, he says, "The Mauna Kea is supposed to be very nice. Built with Rockefeller money, wonderful food, on the big island."

"No, I don't think there. Kauai, the most flowers and the fewest people. We could lie on the beach and watch the surf, the surfers."

Smith is putting on weight, which gives him a vague but puzzlingly effeminate look. No time ever to exercise, he says. He sighs, in a new sad fat way, so that I feel a surge of pity for him. But I want to go to Hawaii.

The father of Catherine's child is unmistakable—and she is right; he is beautiful, a wide-shouldered, darkly tanned black-haired young god. Lying white and fearsome on that whitest of white beaches, we watch him every day. (Of course Smith does not know who he is.) And what he does on the water is truly godlike: he glides along the undercurl of those glistening steep and wickedly breaking waves; he glides, glides—he is astounding, the nerve and balance and grace.

There is really no need to find out his name or speak to him; what on earth would I say? We lie there, Smith with his papers and periodicals, I with my books, our fair well-tended skins turning gently from pink to tan. With awe we watch the boy's magnificent swift performance. And when he walks past us, out of water, we never stare. Although I am able to see at close hand the long marvelous shape of his legs.

And so, in that way, before anyone else, I know what Catherine's son will eventually look like, and I have some idea of what sort of boy he will be.

18 / Women Friends

"Catherine, darling, I *need* that room, the space. I can really use it. I'm sorry if you think I'm selfish. The point is you can't live here and in Mendocino, and you certainly can't live here with a baby. I'm too old for babies. You were the only one I could stand. Catherine, please try to understand. I'm tired of working in stray corners of the house, or in bed. I want a room for nothing but my work. A room of my own. Before you left, I was thinking about renting one. Catherine, I'm a writer, a poet, and in two years I'll be forty. I need my own room."

Late January, in San Francisco, a suddenly warm bright false spring day. False green on the hills of Marin, which Eliza saw as she spoke on the phone to Catherine. What she was looking at when Catherine called. Catherine, although six months pregnant and living in several other places, Mendocino to Big Sur, did not want to move out entirely; she still wanted to keep her room full of clothes and books, magazines, souvenirs. This morning's conversation was the last in a series (Eliza hoped).

She, Eliza, had spoken in a firm, controlled way. Believing herself to be right, to be within her rights, she had stated her case to Catherine much more definitely and clearly than before.

And, in response, Catherine had made sounds of comprehension, even of acceptance.

Why, then, hanging up, did Eliza observe that her strong, stained and unkempt but capable hands were trembling, out of control? Why did she feel herself to be near tears? Was she not supposed to be a writer? Was she supposed to be, for the rest of her life, Catherine's mother?

A month later, a cold, relentlessly wet February, Eliza had her room. A long wide desk, the oak top supported by two small filing cabinets, also oak. All the wood stripped down to a smooth bare whiteness—stripped until Eliza suspected herself of postponing more difficult work: her own difficult poetry. Walls lined with bookcases, a small cupboard of supplies. A table with a double burner, things for coffee. A wide and undraped window that looked out to a wall of dark green wet leaves.

All that remained of Catherine was her narrow girlish bed and, invisible in a closet, some discarded girlish clothes, which Eliza meant to give to the Goodwill. Surely Catherine would never dress like that again?

There was Eliza at her desk, with nothing to keep her from work. Enough money to live on coming in, no terrible bills, no time-consuming lover. And she had "got over" Reed, except for an occasional moment of wonder that she was ever in love with him in the first place.

There she was, with fewer demands and obligations than she had ever known.

From her desk Eliza stared out into the rain and the glistening thick leaves; she was thinking of the year when at just this time it was so hot, thinking of the sound of firecrackers in the unnatural heat. She thought of her hospital job, now remote, of Gilbert Branner. And Miriam—where was she?

A couple of months ago, Miriam had called Eliza, obviously high; but warm, very friendly. Curious about and anxious to see Eliza. And Eliza asked her to come to lunch on her day off. She made a nice chicken salad, rolls, and, remembering Miriam's fondness for sweets, bought pastry in North Beach. And Miriam didn't show up. Eliza felt several things: hurt, irritation and comprehension—high, Miriam simply didn't remember. Still, it was hard to know what to do next, and Eliza had done nothing.

Except to think of Miriam, when she should have been working on a poem.

The phone rang.

Eliza was unable not to answer the phone. Remnants of past urgencies, of Catherine's needs, made her hurry from her desk and across the hall to that jangling black instrument.

At Peggy Kennerlie's soft proper voice, which she had heard every other day that month, Eliza experienced an extreme, exaggerated irritation; she had only to say, Look, I'm working, I can't talk. Peggy was silly and demanding but she was not unreasonable. (Was she?) Instead, invitingly (another old habit), Eliza said, *"Hi."*

"Hi, how are you? Well, you're not going to believe this, but guess what Ted called about this morning. He wants the grapefruit spoons. I mean, I know they were his mother's, but honestly, Liza—"

This had been going on for several months, and Eliza, who hated being called Liza, had almost totally run out of interest. When the Kennerlies had first separated, she had been surprised: the Kennerlies not getting along? (Harry said, "Come on, you're not surprised at all; you're too smart for that. You were never fooled by all that cornball palsy stuff, were you?") She went from surprise to sympathy; she called Peggy often, imagining loneliness; she invited her to supper several times. But all Peggy had wanted to talk about was the property settlement; it was her sense of ownership that was outraged.

Weakly, Eliza said, "Oh, grapefruit spoons?" feeling as she spoke a rush of acute annoyance.

Of course, Peggy went on to make it worse. "As a matter of fact, I'm in town right now," she said, "and would it be okay if I came by for a minute? I've got some drapery samples that I really want to show you— I'm getting all new. Could you throw some peanut butter on a piece of bread, or something?" And she gave her warm, characteristic slightly out-of-place laugh.

Nothing about any of that was new, and so why did Eliza

say furiously, "No, Peggy, for Christ's sake, I'm working."

"Working? What do you mean?"

"I'm writing, for God's sake. And I don't feel like drapery samples, or grapefruit spoons."

"Well." Peggy tried to laugh in her old accustomed way. That failed, and she said exaggeratedly, "Well, I'm *sorry.*" But then, from her prim puritanical mouth, this broke out: "Jesus, Liza, don't you ever do anything you don't want to do?"

"Peggy—Christ, what a question." But, saying that, Eliza's voice cracked.

As did Peggy's as she said, "Well, then. Goodbye."

They both hung up, and just as after her last argument with Catherine, Eliza found that her hands were trembling. She felt near tears. And *why?* This was how she used to feel after early wrenching scenes with Josephine. Hopelessly she thought, I am unable to argue decently with anyone, but I *have* to, obviously, especially with people who get in the way of my working, even if it is a daughter, a mother, an old friend.

Outside, the rain had slackened momentarily, leaving an empty sad gray sky above the Bay and barely visible Marin; everywhere water dripped, and slid down the smooth surfaces of gutters and the slick bark of trees.

And Eliza went on thinking, staring out. Some people, women, were good fighters, she thought. Josephine, Kathleen—and for the first time certain basic similarities between those two occurred to Eliza—or did she simply react to both of them in the same way, with fear?

Why could she never tell Kathleen, for example, how much she disliked her smoking?

Feeling defiant, Eliza dialed the familiar number. "Hello, Kathleen?"

She was greeted with an outburst that even for Kathleen was violent. "*Well.* I suppose you think that's really neat, fixing it up with Miriam and Lawry. Or was it one of your upper-class jokes? Do they both report in to you now, Miss Super-Cunt?

Does Lawry tell you that black snatch is really the greatest, and Miriam going on about white cock?"

"Kathleen." Eliza was surprised to find herself quite calm. "Kathleen, I literally do not know what you're talking about."

"Okay, *Mrs.* Quarles, are you going to tell me you didn't give Lawry Miriam's phone number?"

"I have truly never spoken to Lawry in my life."

"Then how the fuck did he get it?" Kathleen's voice had only slightly subsided.

"Any number of ways. From the business office, for one. From one of the interns she knew. Come on, Kathleen, how many big black girls named Miriam work over there?"

As Kathleen was thinking that out, Eliza battled her own curiosity, and then gave in. She asked, "What makes you think he found her? That they got together?"

Kathleen snorted. "Easiest thing in the world. Miriam hadn't shown up for a week or so. And one day I decided to call Lawry in L.A.—I hadn't heard from him, but that was nothing new. And guess who answered his phone. Black Beauty, right? Of course she hung up as soon as she heard me."

"Well." There was little or nothing more for Eliza to say.

Or for Kathleen, who only muttered, "All I can say is she's welcome to him. What a wimp that Lawry is—they really deserve each other. And he'd be a lot worse with money. Selfish, spoiled and vain—they'll be fighting over the mirror. But Christ, the nerve of that black cunt—"

Eliza at last got back to work.

A few days later a gaudy postcard came to Eliza, from Las Vegas. In Miriam's beautiful handwriting, her impossible grammar and spelling. Translated, it went, "Dear Eliza, this Vegas is something else, I mean. And Lawry is really nice. I like him a lot. Don't tell Kathleen, she don't know anything. With best wishes from your friend, Miriam."

Miriam—Las Vegas? This jarred Eliza, and then it made her smile, if a little sadly, and as in a vision she saw Miriam walking into a club, at night, toward a spotlit table. Miriam in tight satin, with high white boots, a dream outfit. Miriam standing up tall, and beautiful, with flowers in her hair.

19 / Catherine's Baby

By April, when Catherine's baby was due, Catherine was living in Mendocino, with "some friends," with no phone. At unpredictable intervals she called her mother, usually prompted by a frantic postcard from Eliza, who tried to restrain herself—but sometimes an unanticipated maternal anxiety broke through. By the first of May, Eliza found that she was writing postcards every day.

She thought a great deal, really obsessively, of that coming child, who she believed would be a girl. She thought of that line of females, seeing it as an actual line: Josephine, herself, Catherine and now the new baby, a new person. A succession of powerful women, often at war with each other. Daria was somewhere off to the side, not herself a mother, and preoccupied with troubles of her own.

Eliza thought, too, of how young she herself was to become a grandmother, only a couple of years from forty. And Josephine, to be a great-grandmother in her vigorous late fifties? Eliza almost resented the new titles that Catherine was giving them; she almost resented that new woman-to-be.

On a day in the second week in May, Eliza made two phone calls: one to an inn in Mendocino where once she stayed with Harry; another to the Greyhound terminal. And she wrote her final postcard to Catherine: "Cat, I'm coming up to the Little

River Inn. Have dinner with me tomorrow night if you're not busy with a baby or anything. Love. E."

The highway north of the Golden Gate Bridge was too familiar to Eliza for notice as the big bus pressed ahead, and at first she read from a paperback novel—as best she could. But then, sometime past San Rafael, the very idea of "north" became exciting, simply the direction. And, understanding this, Eliza smiled, because of course she was thinking of Maine, of going north to Maine. And how Harry would be amused at that.

She was also thinking of babies; she saw a particular new fat blond baby girl. Was it possible that she could imagine Catherine's child, who was possibly already born? Both were possible, but actually the baby in her mind was Catherine: Catherine just born to Eliza, and instantly adored—although not adored by her father, who seemed both frightened and vaguely repelled by this noisy new infant. Evan.

But Catherine could have a dark child; she had, Eliza believed, at some time mentioned the father: "Really beautiful, with this blue-black hair." Eliza saw, or conjured up, a baby who was dark: a tiny one, screaming, in a pink-trimmed white wicker basket. It was Daria, tended by a nurse and regarded with a kind of distraught alarm by Josephine—who felt, at thirty, too old for this, who already hated her husband, Jason Paulus. A baby regarded with some distaste by Eliza, who was ten, a bookish, nonmaternal little girl. Daria cried her lungs out, and no one knew what to do, until the nurse picked her up. A Scottish nurse, Mrs. Barnes. "She wants her lunch, poor mite. Have you ever seen such a small thing so starved?"

At Cloverdale the lumbering bus turned westward, into hills, past fields and meadows, toward the coast. Eliza watched everything, paying attention; like someone reading, she intently followed the lines of trees, the gray houses, fields, sheep and outcroppings of rock that were the shape of sheep.

The coast, as they emerged to it—turning up to the right, up north—was glorious: green meadows of wildflowers, all yellow and blue, with orange California poppies—meadows that stretched to sheer sudden cliffs of eroded rock and then dropped dramatically down to the sea, the brilliant Pacific, which that day was the deepest azure.

Eliza's room at the inn had just that view, a flowering meadow framed by dark bent cypresses. She sat on her porch and watched a haze of afternoon sunlight out on the water. She sipped some wine, and waited for Catherine.

Who arrived earlier than Eliza would have expected: Catherine, huge and exhausted, stringy-haired, looking pitifully older than her actual eighteen. They embraced, they greeted each other, and Eliza asked if Catherine was hungry. Would she like an early dinner: Yes, actually she was starved.

During their meal, in the inn's pleasant dining room, Catherine consumed two orders of abalone and instructed her mother in Lamaze. The exercises, the breathing, the necessary friend in the delivery room. This last was all set, although at first the hospital had made a fuss, Catherine triumphantly recounted. She seemed to have spent the last several months studying obstetrics, and she spoke familiarly of effacement and dilation, episiotomies and presentations; Eliza felt both ignorant and very slightly bored.

"How was I born? What method?" Catherine wanted to know.

"Well, in 1950 natural childbirth was the thing to do, and so I tried it, but it didn't work out too well."

"Of course not," Catherine pronounced. "It wasn't thorough enough. It was really just a guilt trip that some English guy laid on women."

After dinner Catherine was terribly sleepy, and said that

she would go on home. Her house was less than half a mile away. They agreed to meet in the morning: Catherine would come for breakfast, and then they would take a walk.

That night, very calmly, with no irritation at all, no self-pity or disappointment, Eliza decided that she was unnecessary to this birth: Catherine, or Catherine and her friends, could perfectly cope. And she, Eliza, the grandmother-to-be, would take the bus back to San Francisco.

At breakfast Catherine had a small steak and potatoes and fried eggs; she announced that she was feeling terrific, she really dug being pregnant. Perhaps this would be a ten-month baby? Would be especially handsome and well developed? Eliza agreed; yes, he-she certainly could be. But privately she considered the stronger possibility that Catherine, with all her new medical knowledge, could quite well have miscalculated the date of conception; she had never been good at arithmetic.

It was another dazzling, beautiful day. They walked in the meadows, among the yellow broom, blue lupin, the orange poppies.

"Where do you live, exactly?" Eliza asked.

"Oh, it's over there. Actually, it's not much of a house."

Eliza took the afternoon bus home, and it seemed to take much longer than the six hours of getting to Mendocino.

She had been in her own house for less than an hour, had washed her face and heated some leftover soup, when the telephone rang. It was Catherine's friend, her Lamaze partner—a girl who sounded about twelve years old. Who said that he was born: *he;* Catherine had had a nine-pound boy, "with this terrific thick black hair, and she didn't have a bad time at all—her water—the doctor—her milk—" Catherine would call Eliza tomorrow.

Most unexpectedly, and for the first time in her life, Eliza was hysterical, truly out of rational control; she laughed and cried together, as she had read that hysterical people did, and at the same time she was watching herself, and she felt ridiculous.

Out of rational control: she was seized with strong impulses, which she acted on. From the refrigerator she took a big cold bottle of champagne. (Harry had what he called "a vulgar taste for French bubbly," and he kept her supplied.) She opened the wine, thinking that she had never opened a bottle of champagne before, certainly never drunk it by herself, as she then did.

Glass in hand, she went over to the record player; she put on old favorites. Billie, Bessie Smith, Lena Horne.

All that music sounded jubilant, and stirring; she could not sit still and drink her wine and listen. She began to move all around the downstairs of her house, in time with the livelier songs, in a very private swaying little dance. And she thought, I am dancing a Grandmother Dance. Thought, Have I finally gone mad? But of course she had not; what she felt was wonderful—happiness, relief.

The Grandmother Dance was something that Eliza never told anyone about, not even Harry. There was no way to describe it.

The baby boy, named Dylan, Dylan Quarles, was exceptionally handsome; as Catherine said, he looked just like his father.

And by the time of his first birthday, Catherine was pregnant again, by another "really beautiful" boy.

20 / *Eliza at Forty*

It was much too hot to sleep. Eliza, whose fortieth birthday it would be the following day, and Harry (this trip was his present) lay untouching and far apart on their new, very hard, and preposterously wide bed—in August, in Ixtapanejo. Too hot even to make love; instead they talked through most of the night, murmuring against the heavy tropical stillness.

"We really should have gone to Italy," whispered Harry a little hoarsely. "Ravello in August, it would be perfect. Look, why don't we go back to Mexico City tomorrow? We could get on a plane to Rome, and then—"

Eliza laughed softly, exhaustedly. "Harry, darling, I'm at the end of my stamina for flying. I could *not* fly to Rome tomorrow, or the next day. Take me to Ravello when I'm fifty, okay?"

"Sure, 1980. Who'll be alive by then? And someone will have bought Ravello, some terrible oil person—" In part, he was referring to the fact that their hotel (they were in the same one that they had come to before, the time they met) had been bought by a Texas oil billionaire, who had horrifyingly renovated it: doubled and crowded the number of units, brought in these uncomfortable "modern" beds and mechanized the service, or nearly so—the maids' bells often didn't work, nor did the garish new ice machine in the bar.

With the tips of her fingers, Eliza touched his distant thigh; an enormous effort was required for that reach, and the slight touch seemed intensified, immense. "Harry, it was perfect to come here," she said. "I would have wanted—"

Impossible even to finish any sentence. Words fell heavily between them; their bodies lay heavily in the sweating sheets. Earlier a mosquito had buzzed around the room, as loud as a bombing raid, until Harry got up and, after a prolonged and clumsy chase, managed to kill it with a slipper against the bathroom mirror.

"Besides," Eliza continued, "Smith and Daria—"

Who were to arrive the next day. In Smith's plane; along with his other innovations, the Texan had put in an airstrip.

"Inside my head," murmured Harry, "I'm dying to make love to you, but—"

"Yes, I know." She felt the same; in her mind, she remembered Harry's hands and mouth, while her body was oppressed with humid air, with the hot thick night, over-whelmed with sick-sweet flower smells and the distant droning of the somnolent sea. Not a rustle in the palm fronds outside their window, or in the dusty thick hibiscus leaves. No breeze.

Eliza tried to remember, to imagine, to *feel*, the lake in Maine, the lapping cool, the blue. But she couldn't. She was relentlessly here.

Toward dawn they both slept dreamlessly, heavily; waking was like coming out from under massive drugs, anesthesia. Harry rolled toward her and said, "Happy birthday, love." A quick dry kiss.

"Forty. Jesus," said Eliza.

Laboriously they got out of bed and washed and dressed. "I feel more like ninety-two," Eliza said.

Texan know-how only goes so far: the lovely open dining room was quite unchanged—was surrounded still with a wild profusion of tropical blooms, and looked out to the flat still sea.

Breakfast was the same: cold fruit and colder bacon, hot tortillas. Strong coffee, which made both Harry and Eliza feel much better.

"I wonder if I'll ever make this movie," Harry said. "The one starting with you, at the Kennerlies, in the rain. You wouldn't believe how often I think of that, and of us here." He stared at her as though she were new, with his passionate pale eyes.

She laughed. "No, I wouldn't. When would you have time?" In the last five years, Harry had made four movies, all but one major successes—the failure, of course, being his favorite. And Eliza's: to her it was like an especially loved poem that no one would buy. (Eliza had recently published one small collection of poems, in a paperback edition.)

Harry continued to stare. "At times you're very close to being beautiful," he said.

Unembarrassed—she was used to Harry, used and most fond—Eliza laughed again. "Don't lose your head. Maybe sometimes pretty, but today I doubt it. Forty-year-old tired person. Daria is beautiful—wait till you see her."

"I love those fine lines at the corners of your eyes, especially when you're all nice and brown."

"Harry, couldn't we get some more coffee? I need some."

"Sure. But isn't it strange without Otto stalking around?"

"Like Alec Guinness. You see? I remember everything you say."

"I should hope so; it's all immortal."

The sky was strange and yellowish, intensely still. Heavy, but with no promise of a break, of rain or storm. And the water was a curious yellow-gray, shining and endlessly flat. A huge white boat, someone's yacht, was anchored there, beside which the slow-moving fishing boats looked smaller still; they crawled across the water like ants.

"Even the ocean looks hot today," Eliza remarked.

"I know, we should have gone to Maine. We still could—we could—"

"*Harry,* I can't fly any more. Not this week."

"When do you think Smith and Daria will get here?"

"I don't know. I guess sometime this afternoon."

"I wonder why two rooms."

"Oh, Smith being grand, I suppose. All that Washington stuff is going to his head."

"You are hard on him."

"That's what Josephine says."

Harry mused. "It must be some violent and submerged sexual attraction between you."

Eliza laughed.

Midmorning. Harry and Eliza were down on the beach when Smith and Daria appeared—Smith and Daria and ("My God," Eliza whispered) Dylan, Catherine's tall black-haired son, now two years old. Daria came first, walking buoyantly, wearing white lace over something dark and brief; she was leading Dylan by the hand. Then Smith, somewhat portly, proud, and then a young Mexican girl, whose function seemed to be the care of Dylan—she was carrying some of his accoutrements: a small shirt, a boat, a hat.

"Well—" They all moved quickly toward each other, exchanging kisses, words of greeting, as though surprised, in the pounding sun, there on the sand.

The only true surprise was, of course, Dylan; startled, Harry and Eliza wondered if he had been adopted by Daria and Smith, or if this was just a trip for him. Their idea of a treat for Eliza's birthday?

Smith, who was always brighter and more intuitive than Eliza believed, read both their minds, and cleared up the confusion: "Dylan's first plane trip," he said. "Catherine sends love; she's busy planting potatoes." In an awkwardly well-meant gesture, he tousled Dylan's extremely beautiful black silk hair (as Eliza thought, Ah, you don't like children either, do you, now?).

So Dylan was a treat for her birthday. Her grandson, for

her fortieth. This suddenly seemed to Eliza terribly funny, and she began to laugh, rather out of control. "I don't know," she at last got out. "The heat—"

They all walked toward a group of white (new-painted, bright) slatted wooden chairs, some beach umbrellas, and they arranged themselves there, more or less protected from the sun. The Mexican girl took Dylan down to the water.

The chairs were in a row, facing the sea; next to Eliza, Daria said, "I feel as though we were on the porch in Maine." She was most beautiful at this moment in her life: deep gold eyes, smooth skin, her fine black feathery hair a cloud around her small and shapely head.

Looking at Daria, and then at Smith, whose hair was gray now (he was as distinguished as Josephine had imagined he would be), Eliza sensed that this time, these months and maybe years, would be pivotal in their married life; they were on a happy plateau. Smith was happy with his money and his Washington connections; Daria was visibly happy, too. (With Smith? No matter.) Daria was no longer obsessed.

"Maine," Harry is saying. "I feel that it's some mysterious place from which I'm forever prohibited. Smith, have you ever been to Maine?"

"Well, yes—in fact, we were married there."

"Ten years ago." Daria's face shone, for whatever reasons.

"Well, you see?" Harry spread his competent knotty hands before him, as though he were helpless.

"Darling, we could go to Maine," Eliza said. "It's just never worked out. You don't have time when I'm going there, or we go somewhere else."

"Yes, and other places that you like all remind you of Maine. A sort of imprinting seems to have gone on."

Liking his word, Eliza looked at him with an astonished pleasure; Harry was a delight—her true best friend.

It was the best time that those four oddly assorted people had ever had together. As two couples, they did not really know each other very well. They had met for dinner a few times in San

Francisco, always at Jack's, the favorite restaurant of both Harry and Smith. (They had that much in common.) But those meetings had been stiff, rather formal, and Eliza had wondered nervously what Smith (always the unknown) made of her connection with Harry. He must have known that they were lovers, but did he then wonder at the off-and-on quality of their connection? Could he *not* think, Well, why don't they marry, or come to some "appropriate" solution? It was not so much that she cared about Smith's opinions, or his possible judgments, as that she did not want to be uncomfortably aware of them. Or so she told herself.

In consideration of Smith's possible prejudices, it had been decided (by Harry and Eliza) that her birthday lunch should be in the dining room, not in their favorite place, which was the beach shack restaurant.

Margaritas, guacamole. Lobsters, champagne. The champagne from a hamper, imported by Smith in his plane. Eliza winced a little at that gesture, and then forced herself to think, Oh, well.

They sat on the gorgeously flowered open deck, the lovely airy space, and watched the sea.

"What nice wine," Eliza said at last to Smith, realizing that she should have said it before.

"I just bought my fifteenth copy of your book," he answered, quite startlingly.

"Oh, really? Smith, how nice."

"Yes, I give it to people. I don't know what to say to poets, so I just buy the books and sort of spread them around." But he looked very pleased with himself, conscious of having done and said the right thing. And then he said what was even more surprising to Eliza: "Get yourself a new photographer, though. That picture doesn't do you justice."

He looked at her in a plump and kindly way.

"Smith," she began, and then broke off. She laughed and looked at Harry, as though for help. "This may be my favorite birthday," she finally said.

They all smiled in pleased and surprised ways at each other; they concentrated on lobsters.

"My God," Smith suddenly exclaimed a few minutes later; he had just looked at his watch. "Time to phone." He got up and rushed from the room. Gone.

"Washington. Every day." In a new way Daria laughed. "I don't even know who he's talking to."

They all laughed, until the sound of their laughter was broken by a sudden clap of thunder from the sea. They looked out toward the gate of rocks, the western end of the bay, and there were enormous black clouds, massed and menacing.

As suddenly as the clap of thunder sounded, they were deluged with rain: huge drops, bucketfuls thrown from the sky, beating down palm fronds, bending heavy hibiscus leaves, crumpling the big flowers to the wilted shapes of bright wet scarves, hanging limp.

The rain washed the air, bringing coolness.

Daria and Eliza looked at each other. And Harry interrupted what they were going to say: "It's just like storms in Maine. Please don't tell me that, I *know*."

"Well, not exactly," Daria told him seriously. "But a little. That's something I miss in California. Thunderstorms."

Harry stared at her (into her, she felt), so that when she looked up at him she blushed a little. Their first sexual moment.

The rain stopped.

In the sudden cool there was only the sound of dripping water, from fronds to leaves, roofs down to gutters, to earth. Daria shivered.

Harry turned to Eliza, away from Daria; he said, "Shouldn't we—"

"Yes."

The three of them left the dining room together, and Eliza experienced a wild strange sense that they were all going to bed together. (Would Harry like that? Would she? Well, no.) They left Daria at her door, and continued to their room.

"You're right, she's *very* beautiful."

"You never saw it?"

"Not so much."

"I wonder who on earth Smith—"

"Our President, of course."

They both laughed, now half undressed.

"How crazy bringing Dylan. He's probably in Daria's room. Her excuse," Eliza said.

"You just don't like two-year-olds."

"Neither does Smith."

"I have a hunch it was Daria's idea."

"You're probably right, you usually are. It makes me hate you."

"You know, you're lovelier naked than with clothes on, much—"

In her room, where in a cot near her bed Dylan lay asleep, Daria took out a piece of paper, and a pen. She wrote: "My darling, Reed, I am wild about—insane—"

21 / Reed and Daria

Early evening, late fall, in Amsterdam. On a terrace, together, both very beautiful, Reed and Daria were considering how to end their love affair. Again.

Below them the dark canal reflected evening lights. A boat had just passed by: a broad glass-topped excursion cruise that disturbed the surface of the water, so that the reflections were all agitated, the lights all danced. As, on the tables, candles flickered in the cool north fall breeze. The people in the tourist boat could not see the couples dining on the terrace, could not see Reed and Daria near the edge, but they received an impression of romantic opulence, of mystery.

The other diners stared intermittently at the exceptionally handsome couple; Reed, who had always been beautiful, was used to it; not stared at, he would feel cut off from air. Daria took attention less for granted; it still made her shy. She would rather that they were alone; earlier she suggested dinner in her room at the Amstel (the hotel where they met, with Smith, all those years ago). Reed this time was staying at a cheaper place: a tiny upstairs room, but in a beautiful converted house, on one of the loveliest canals.

He said that he would rather go out. "I'll behave better in public," he said.

In fact, Daria was quite unused to being beautiful. At

college she was a pretty girl, but so was everyone else. And then a "beautiful bride" (but not really). And then, years of tears, almost crazy with crying, too thin. Then she stopped crying, almost stopped caring about anything at all, and she got away from doctors. She fell in love (or saw that she had always been in love) with Reed, the family friend. Who loved her, too (although at first not so much), who said that she was lovely. And then she was; even she could see it, her extraordinary beauty.

"What I don't understand" Reed said, with a tight gesture of his hands, a tightening in his voice, "is why we have to be so absolute. We've tried it before. It never works out."

"I don't know why either," Daria agreed. "I only know it's true. Seeing each other 'sometimes' doesn't work out. It ends by being my whole life."

He gulped at wine, a famous burgundy, which he could barely taste. "It's always seemed so harsh, so *uncivilized* to me," he said. "Breaking up, the way people do. One day in bed, the next not speaking."

This had been said with such weariness, the fatigue of too many affairs, a lifetime of love affairs. Which Daria recognized. "I've never 'broken up' with anyone before," she tartly reminded him. "And I don't mean not to speak. Of course not."

He had intuitively, as always, read her mind, and her negative judgment. "I know, I've made a sort of career of love affairs," he admitted. "I guess I should have been a woman. Supposedly that's okay for them."

She smiled. "Not any more."

"Well, anyway. I always hate endings. Girls even seem to like them." He was thinking of Eliza, whom Daria did not know about. Reed was discreet—Eliza, too.

"I don't like this," Daria said honestly. "It was much more fun to begin. If I hadn't been so frightened—"

"Well, my God, here we are in Amsterdam, where we've always meant to come. Why not rebegin, instead? You're my great love, you know that."

This had been said mockingly, but it was true; Daria knew

this, and she felt an inexplicable pity for him. He was almost forty, heavier and less beautiful than he used to be. She said, "I love you, too," being both kind and polite, if a little naïve. "But I've changed too much. I need some kind of freedom. I don't know—"

"Will you divorce Smith?"

"Probably. I'm not sure."

"Beautiful Daria, I don't understand you at all."

"I don't understand myself. I just know that I need to change things in my life. It's odd: sometimes I feel as old as Josephine, more like her sister than Eliza's." Daria was wearing soft pale wool clothes, fine and filmy, in loose folds around her slender neck, her shoulders. Now with a gesture of self-sufficiency, she pulled her collar close.

"Are you cold?"

"No, maybe tired."

"Why aren't you sadder? Christ, Daria, think how we've been."

"Reed, I'm sorry. And I do think."

"In any case, we need more wine. A nice white, with dessert?"

"I really don't want dessert."

"Well, we could have the wine anyway. It's so incredibly beautiful here. Enough to break your heart."

They had spent the afternoon walking around the city—to which, as a treat, or possibly a test, Daria came alone, Smith being both busy and permissive. And Reed simply arrived, that morning. They went to the Van Gogh Museum, and had lunch there, at its terrace snack bar. And then they walked: past brilliant flower stalls and elegant dark stores, high narrow brick houses that seemed to lean toward the canals, walking always along by the dark smooth water, with yellow leaves adrift. The lovely gentle city where, all those years ago, they first met and did not then fall in love. Walking and arguing, getting nowhere but both trying to be nice, to be kind and fair.

Another glass-topped and brightly lit tourist boat slowly passed, in the dark, a barge full of craning people.

The wine arrived and Daria politely sipped at it. She was thinking that Reed had begun to drink too much. It showed in the puffiness, though slight, around his eyes.

"I wonder when you'll fall in love with someone else," he speculated, with a narrow look at her.

"Maybe never. You know, I'm not like you, or even much like Eliza. I should never have married so young, and maybe not at all. I don't like people much, just children. And animals." Daria was exhausted with the effort of this speech, and the whole day of talking, but she was a little excited, too; she had begun to gain a tiny sense of direction.

Self-absorbed, and growing sadder with more wine, Reed barely listened. "Sometimes I feel like some kind of carrier," he told her. "Some kind of plague. Why am I so often someone's last affair? I thought I was good at being in love."

"You are. It's me who isn't," she brought out. "That's the whole problem with us. Love is not important to me. In fact, sometimes 'madly in love' just seems to mean 'dying to fuck each other.' "

Reed had at times made the same observation—or, rather, reluctantly admitted it to his mind. Still, she had shocked him badly: Daria did not say "fuck."

Four years earlier, on another fall day, in San Francisco, Daria was standing on a street corner, and she thought of Reed (the family friend). She and Smith had come up to town for the weekend to a view-filled corner suite at the Mark; that morning, coming out into the sunlight, Smith had said, "Reed's place must be around here somewhere." "Oh, really?" "Yes, at the end of some alley. Well, there's my cab. I can't drop you somewhere?" "No, thanks, I want to walk for a while."

And she did; she walked around in the brilliant clear fall

sunlight. She looked down Sacramento Street to the Bay, and the Bay Bridge. Everything shone, wherever she looked. The narrow town houses were so elegant, perfectly kept, and the nurses and children in Huntington Park were beautiful, well kempt. Rich tourists gawked from their over-sized cars, but in that heady air everyone looked blessed.

Aware of a dizzying excitement in her blood, Daria began to walk in a certain direction, as though guided toward an address she did not know. Down a street that led north, looking toward the Golden Gate, Marin County, turning in to an alley. Past some terrible new greenish houses, miserably constructed, to a small and decrepit shingled cottage.

It was Reed's cottage; having moved into town from Stinson Beach, he had thumbtacked a tattered white card to the door, bearing his name. Her heart stuck at the top of her throat, but at the same time she was sure of her direction; Daria knocked.

"Daria, well, what a lovely surprise." Actually he had meant to go out, but at least Daria had missed the girl who had just left, angrily. At Daria's knock, Reed had imagined the girl returning to make up. "Well," he said, with an effort, nevertheless, "may I give you some coffee? I'm afraid it's sort of a mess around here."

Like a polite child, Daria nodded; not seeing anything, really, she was dimly aware of "things," probably beautiful, darkly cluttered in a narrow room, and she was violently aware of Reed: gleaming sleek blond hair, wide blue eyes, fine mouth. Long perfect hands, small bare feet.

He was asking her something, from the kitchen.

"Yes, a little milk, please."

He sat down across from her, hiding restlessness. He repeated, "Well, this is a lovely surprise. How's Smith? He must be pleased about the way things are going."

"Oh, yes, very; fine. We're staying at the Mark."

"Oh, really—how nice. You and Smith are sort of my

neighbors, then. Temporarily." What about her was making him so nervous?

"Reed, I came to tell you. I'm absolutely in love with you. Mad. I can't live without you."

He had heard these words before, several times. Something about him, perhaps some deep passivity, invited them. He was used to women professing love, and also certain men. Evan Quarles following him around, staring and silent. Still, he was not blasé, and he was too kind to take anyone's love for granted. Daria had touched him deeply, even thrilled him.

"Daria, beautiful girl, you don't know what you're saying, nor what you'd be getting in for, with me," he said to her.

She was sitting with her knees close together, hands clasped on her lap. As he spoke, she flinched very slightly, tightening her hands, closing knees; then she said, "I do know, or I can imagine. A lot of trouble, probably?"

He smiled; how extremely pretty she was! "Trouble, or worse. And there's your marriage: I like Smith." As he said this, Reed realized that he did not like Smith very much, not really, but did he really like anyone? He had often wondered.

"I don't care. Not about anything."

Tears next; Reed knew the sequence. Speaking very kindly, he said, "Look, I'll go put my shoes on, and we'll go out and get some air, okay?"

She was sitting there docilely, not looking at him, and not crying, when he went into his bedroom. He hunted around for his socks, found his shoes, put them all on and then got up and went over to the wardrobe to comb his hair before the mirror.

Looking into the glass, he saw, reflected from the doorway—Daria, perfectly naked and absolutely beautiful.

He said, "Daria, good Christ," and felt tears at his eyes.

That day ended in a vermilion November sunset; warm color spilled over the western horizon, at the sea, beyond the

Golden Gate; the rest of the sky was cool and clear and slowly darkening, flecked with pale evening stars.

Daria whispered, "Our bed smells of the sea."

"Yes," and Reed sighed, feeling a sort of pity for her—for her innocence, her new love.

They lay there, their hands clasped limply between them.

And then, breaking the spell (and destroying his pleasurable moment of pity), Daria laughed. "I'd better bathe," she said, in a practical way that Reed found upsetting. This lovely, most curious girl will probably hurt me, he thought. And then, for years, he forgot that premonition.

Years of stray afternoons of love (actually fewer, perhaps, than in most illicit love affairs: in curious ways, they both avoided the real encounter). Breathless and desperate telephone calls, letters, telegrams. Magic and madness. A few laughs. For Daria there was the miracle of novelty; surely no one had ever felt this? For Reed there was a strange sad sense of finality; of being finally and completely "in love."

"You're so beautiful—"

"Tomorrow, can you—?"

"No, I guess not until Friday."

"Can you wait?"

"No—"

"Nor I."

"When you laugh, my skin feels lacy, like light through leaves."

Until Daria began to tire of the sheer weight of such intensity, and to say that they should stop. End. Not see each other.

Until Amsterdam.

. . .

After dinner, that night in Amsterdam, they took a cab to the Amstel. And they were silent, all that distance, over bridges and canals.

Reed got out with her, but Daria gestured to the driver to remain. "Reed, darling, I'm exhausted, and you're a little drunk. Come over for breakfast, will you?" She laughed in a light way that to Reed was alarmingly uncaring.

He found the only possible rebellious gesture to be a dismissal of the cab: he would walk the considerable distance to his own canal, his small hotel. Also, perhaps he would sober up somewhat (and besides he was really low on money).

The next day the papers announced that the Vice-President (U.S.) had resigned. Tax evasions. Bribes. All over the Amstel dining room, at breakfast, this news was read and digested, along with the excellent Dutch coffee and rolls and cheese.

Daria, whose mood that day for whatever reason was very high, was entirely pleased. She and Reed did not have a paper; they did not feel a need for further details. Daria was eating a lot; she exclaimed, "Oh, isn't this lovely!" looking out through long windows to the strong Dutch sunlight on leaves, and trees and vines.

"Breakfast is wonderful, or—" Reed had noticed that her golden eyes have flecks of darker gold; were they new? What did this mean?

"Oh, everything. Breakfast, and that Greek V.-P. He must be like my father, that Greek shit." Daria laughed—to Reed, chillingly.

"You dislike Greeks?"

"Of course not; simply, how could Nixon have chosen a decent person?"

Curiously: "I didn't know you cared about politics." He cannot remember an even vaguely political conversation with Daria.

"Oh, but I do. I once spent a whole year planning to kill the P."

"P.?"

"The President. Isn't that funny?" Daria laughed with the relief of one who has made a ludicrous confession: of course no one would believe her.

"That doesn't sound like you." But then, he reflected, neither did what she has more recently been saying: I can't see you any more; love is not important to me.

Across the room from them, alone at a smaller table, was an American, probably a businessman, reading the Paris *Herald*. He was handsome in a burly, weathered way, large and dark; the exact opposite to Reed's attractiveness, Daria thought. And she wondered: Would I enjoy a man like that? He me? And she smiled. Am I going to be promiscuous—is that next? But as quickly as she thought all that she realized that she was not attracted to that other man, or really, any more, to anyone. Reed would be her last lover.

However, she wanted to test her powers, and so she made a small bet with herself: I bet that I can make him turn around, and I will smile, and in a few minutes he will get up and give us (give me) his Paris *Herald* as he leaves the room.

The man turned around to Daria, who smiled. In a hurried way he got up and pushed money onto a tray; magnetized, he crossed the room, and he said, "I thought you folks might like to see this paper." He smiled briefly to Reed, and then fully at Daria. He flashed stained teeth and hard opaque eyes. A man who would murder his wife, for gain, or if he tired of her, is what Daria read in his grimace; perhaps he had?

"Oh, thank you, how wonderful," she trilled quickly, icily. Reed looked across at her, puzzled.

The man, who was also disconcerted, was saying something about good old Ted.

"Ted who?" Daria asked.

Reed scowled, and the strange man hurried off.

"Well, in the first place, I didn't want the bloody paper," Daria explained, once he was gone.

"I wonder why not. More coffee? You did know that 'Ted' is the V.-P.?"

"No. I don't care."

Reed opened the paper, and Daria checked her new pale lipstick in a mirror.

22 / *Eliza and Kathleen*

After their conversation about Miriam and Lawry, and Kathleen's hurled accusations, Eliza did not call Kathleen; but as though nothing had happened, Kathleen continued, at intervals, to call. Nor did she seem to mind that Eliza didn't say much; she seemed totally incurious about Eliza's life, or perhaps to be operating on her old assumptions: sexy rich indolent Eliza would never change. But she, Kathleen, had moved into a women's commune, in the Mission District.

And one day—rather a surprise—she invited Eliza to come over. Very curious, Eliza said she would.

Getting ready, in her bedroom, in a space of faint spring sun, Eliza considered that sometimes what-to-wear assumes the proportions of a much larger problem. In her bra and tights, she could come to no decision. *They*, the frightening unknown new friends of Kathleen's, she imagined as stern and judgmental; they would be wearing genuinely old Levis—or, worse, harsh new ones. Should she wear her old Levis—or old gray slacks?

Kathleen, turned down by all the medical schools of her choice, had furiously decided to be a vet. "Fuck them all, I really dig animals anyway. Fuck people." She had gone to the school at Davis, and got her degree. She now worked in a pet hospital out on Army Street, and she lived with four other women, feminists, "and some kids and five cats" on a small street in the Mission District. In ten minutes she was stopping by to get Eliza.

What to wear, going there.

What would I wear if I were meeting Josephine for lunch? This Zenish question appeared in Eliza's mind (as those other, not unrelated imperatives once appeared to Daria), and she thought, Of course, my gray suede pants and new gray boots. An outfit of which Josephine would not approve, but in which Eliza felt herself to be defined, established. Just now they were her favorite clothes, and why should she wear less for Kathleen and her friends? Why condescend in the dirty Levis that she wears for refinishing furniture?

Also, she thought defensively, if there was the slightest hinted remark about the expensiveness of suede, she could tell the truth: the pants cost twenty-five dollars. Bought in Rome, on her last trip with Harry.

(But Rome?)

Gray pants, black sweater. Was she trying to look severe? *serious?* She added a flimsy bright silk scarf.

And then, since Kathleen was not yet due, she went down to get the mail.

Bills, advertisements and a letter from the *Gotham,* a new and highly successful *Vogue-Bazaar* kind of magazine (more "literary" than either). To whom she had sent a long new poem. "We love it—a full page—five hundred dollars."

All her ambivalence about that glossy magazine vanished, and Eliza experienced a moment of pure delight: they loved it—a full page—and so much money—so much more than anyone had ever paid for a poem of hers.

. . .

Now it was time for Kathleen, who was always prompt. It would be a considerable mistake, Eliza decided, to tell her about the *Gotham*. Much better not.

"Well, you do look neat," Kathleen commented with uncharacteristic friendliness as Eliza stepped into her battered car. Kathleen was wearing the hard dark Levis that Eliza had feared, and a sort of lumberjack plaid coat; she did not look "neat" but she did look content. She looked hard-working. Her graying brown-gold hair was tied back in a bun; her mouth was wide and pale, and firmer than before. Her eyes were lined and tired and at the same time very much alive. She went on, "You are a pleasure to see, Mrs. Quarles. Sometimes I forget how the other half lives, and looks." But this was said with none of her old anger, and Eliza wondered if middle age, or nearly, was mellowing Kathleen.

Then all Kathleen's familiar rage returned: driving across town, she was a continuous explosion of pure fury. "Fucking trucks—buses—cabs— Look, a goddam movie crew. Our fucking mayor can't get enough of that stuff, can he. Will you look at that *building?* A bloody packing crate. Manhattan, here we come. Look, lady, move your fucking Cadillac along."

The house, finally and violently arrived at, was a rakish small cottage on a steep and narrow cobbled street.

"It must be the last cobbled street in the city?" asked Eliza, getting out nervously.

"They're taking the cobbles out next week. Look your last."

Inside the cottage were several small rooms, in total chaos. Clothes books toys cats food. Trash. Cat shit. All scattered everywhere. Following Kathleen, Eliza picked her way through distrustfully, aware (ashamed) of the middle-classness of her reaction, and already somewhat discouraged; she had meant to come and admire a new way of life.

In the kitchen three people were sitting at a large table. Two women and a little boy. One of the women was wiry, dark-haired; the other was soft and blond. The little boy was wiry, too, and dark; he was visibly his mother's son.

Introductions: the dark woman is Lena; Angie, the blond; and Jared, the child. Saying "Hi" all around, Eliza realized that she was very slightly disappointed; having imagined—and, to a certain extent, feared—a larger group, she was braced for just that. She had, in fact, expected a sort of inquisition. (Josephine? She had a quick flash, a film-frame of her mother standing at the doorway, facing out to the porch, in Maine; Josephine severe and censorious. Had she been ready for Josephine?)

Whereas, the conversation was quite ordinary, rather mild. Where to shop, since the Safeway (cheapest) was being boycotted by the United Farm Workers (Chavez). The pain of IUD insertions (Angie). The inhumane suffering of cats in heat (Kathleen). The novelty of that particular neighborhood, the cobbles (Eliza).

Only the little boy made a certain amount of trouble; he wanted to go to the park; he insisted that it was time to go. They had promised. He turned to his mother, "Mother—"

"*Lena,*" she corrected. "And Angie's going to take you to the park."

"No, I want you to come."

"Angie—"

"No, you, *Lena*—"

In the end, all three of them went, Jared between Lena and Angie, holding both their hands.

"We want him to relate to all of us," Kathleen explained. "To be all his parents, less of an exclusive thing with Lena."

"It must be sort of hard."

"It is, for everyone."

Another thing that Eliza was slowly reacting to (or recognizing her own reaction), along with the extraordinary mess and the quite ordinarily nice young women, was the visible poverty in which they were living. It was all meager and shabby and uncomfortable; the kitchen shelves held a sparse array of big dented cans of cheap food brands, and on the floor beans spilled out from large paper sacks. Eliza would have liked to ask about the economics of their life; what she would *really* have liked was to give them a lot of money. (And, seeing this impulse, feeling its strength, she had a flashed vision of Daria: Daria giving her money to poor women, to everyone, and she felt great tenderness for her sister.)

"Well," said Kathleen, "care for more coffee?"

"Yes." (Although it has been terrible, weak and bitter.)

"We're living in a very ideological way," Kathleen more or less announced. And she went on to explain some of what Eliza had wondered about. "I'm the only one who really works," she said. "I mean for money. Lena's on welfare, she's a sculptor— and Angie gets unemployment, she wants to be a mail-carrier. We all pool what we have, but then we often take in other women—women who're just out of jail, or who just can't find places. Things like that."

Rather helplessly, Eliza breathed out, "Wow, that's really *good.*"

Kathleen could no more accept praise than she could (probably) money, and she said, "Well, it's not all that fucking good. There's a lot left to do." And then she asked, "Well, tell me about your people. Harry? Daria and Smith? And *Catherine*—how is Catherine?"

Eliza smiled, but rather sadly. "Catherine's fine, but she's got two babies now. They all seem terribly happy; she's down at a place in the Santa Cruz Mountains, but still—"

"You've always been hard on her. You know, you're more like Josephine than you admit. Catherine was supposed to act out your fantasies, a good college and all that, just the way Josephine was ambitious for you."

This was quite true, but Eliza did not like to admit or to

talk about it; she was, in fact, terribly disappointed in Catherine. And so she said, "Daria is really terrific now."

Kathleen was curiously uninterested in Daria's being terrific; she frowned and asked, "How's Smith?"

"Oh, he's fine. Busy—you know."

"I guess Daria watches him pretty closely?"

Knowing more or less what was meant, Eliza still asked, "How do you mean?"

"Well, he's obviously a prime suicide candidate. As Daria would be the first to know. The third husband in your group to go that way. Just the suggestion could be very strong, with him."

Faintly: "Of course I've thought of that," Eliza said.

Then, perhaps fortunately, a cat began to yowl, and then another cat. Kathleen frowned, more concerned than annoyed. "Jesus, poor things. I'm spaying the female tomorrow."

"Suppose she's already pregnant?" Eliza asked unthinkingly.

"So? You've got something against abortions for cats?"

At this they both could laugh. And, for the moment, they forgot about Smith, and his potential for self-destruction.

A little later, Kathleen asked, "Did you hear about Miriam and Lawry?" From the glee in her voice, Eliza understood that the news would not be good.

"No."

"Well, I read in some Hollywood column they broke up. He's got some new Hawaiian chick. Christ, he really likes them dark."

"But what happened to Miriam?"

"Shit, how would I know? She's probably a hooker in Vegas by now."

"Kathleen! That's horrible—how can you?"

"Look, Eliza, I know a lot of women to worry about. I can't add one more black hooker to my list. And you're really nutty about black women. Why don't you try living with one? See how you like it."

"I don't much want to live with anyone. But you could really be wrong about Miriam. She could have found someone else, too. Guys were always following her around."

"Oh, who gives a shit about Miriam, anyway. I never think about her. Lawry either. All that's dead."

But for Eliza all that past was continuously present. She could see Miriam in a stiff white lab coat that camouflaged her awkwardly top-heavy body, crossing the street to the hospital. She could see Gilbert Branner, stroking his hair, not speaking to Miriam, not ever. She said to Kathleen, "I really cared about Miriam."

"You care too much, about everyone. I think basically you and Daria are a lot alike."

Kathleen was often correct, but did she have to give out so much truth? Eliza pondered this, feeling both bruised and cowardly. And sad about lost Miriam.

She decided that she had been there with Kathleen for too long, perhaps heard too much, and so she got up to go.

But at that moment Lena and Angie were heard coming in the front door, and then walking back to the kitchen. "We left him in the park with Carol—she's got Tony there," they explained; and Angie said to Eliza, "You're not going? Stay and have some more coffee—we've hardly seen you."

Oh, they like me, Eliza thought, quite pleased and a little surprised. She accepted more coffee, and they all smiled warmly at each other. Except Kathleen, who was spewing smoke, then stopping to cough.

"I read a poem of yours in the *Nation* a couple of months ago," Lena said. "I really liked it."

This was so unexpected (these women had time for reading poetry?) and so genuinely *nice* that Eliza was more or less thrown off balance, and she said what she had been holding submerged in her mind all morning—what she had not meant to say. "A funny thing happened to me today," she said. "A couple of months ago, I saw a copy of that new magazine, the *Gotham*, in my dentist's office [she noted that she had felt it necessary to explain that she did not buy it] and I saw some poetry in it, so I sent them a new one, long, about five stanzas, and they're buying it! For five hundred dollars."

"Oh, really? How terrific—that's really great—five hundred—wow—terrific," said Lena and Angie.

"Some fancy dentist you must go to" was all that Kathleen said. But Eliza told herself that Kathleen only sounded so gruff, so cross; Kathleen was really a warm and kindly person; she had always said this to herself, about Kathleen.

"I was really pleased," Eliza admitted. "I know it's a silly magazine, and all that. Still."

"I think it's wonderful," said Angie.

Soon after that, Eliza left; she went home on a series of buses, having been scrupulously directed by Kathleen.

The next day she still felt high, warmed by that pleasant success, and also warmed by what seemed a friendly visit with Kathleen. Meeting those nice feminist women.

More or less in that spirit, she telephoned Kathleen, meaning to thank her, to say what a nice time she had had.

Kathleen listened, but so silently, with such an almost audible stiffness, that Eliza, to herself, sounded ridiculous, banal—a silly woman mouthing politenesses. She could hear Kathleen emitting smoke, and her cough.

"Well," Kathleen said at last. "It must have been quite a day for you. Slumming in your grey suede pants and bragging about slick magazines. You may not know it, *Mrs.* Quarles, but to some people five hundred dollars is a hell of a lot of money. Welfare checks don't come to anything like that."

Thrown off base—a generally pacific person being attacked by a practiced fighter—Eliza felt her mind actually reel, and she answered foolishly. "Those are very cheap pants. I got them in Rome for twenty-five dollars."

"Rome!" Kathleen shrieked the syllable. "Rome, yes, on one of your frequent trips abroad. Maybe you can get a job as a foreign correspondent for the *Gotham*."

"Kathleen—really—"

"Really, you come over here and condescend to some very nice women, with your unimportant five-hundred-dollar checks."

"Kathleen, five hundred dollars is very important to me. I need it, and I know it's a lot of money." But as she said this, Eliza's voice broke, and she felt as guilty as though what she was saying were not true. Her hands were trembling, and she managed to say, "Kathleen, I hate this conversation, I'll call you later." She hung up, just before she began to cry.

Unfair. Kathleen's attack was totally unfair (wasn't it?); unfair, unkind and unprovoked.

But Eliza was unable to dismiss those charges against herself, and in her mind she continued to defend herself against them.

She had worn expensive-looking clothes: but the other choices were not good either—a skirt seemed wrong, and dirty Levis really condescending.

(Kathleen, I was not condescending to your friends; I *liked* them, a lot.)

Maybe mentioning the *Gotham* and the poem was wrong, but I did it out of good feeling, Eliza said to herself (to Kathleen). Sharing good news with new friends.

And I do need the money, Kathleen. It's true that I know some rich people—Smith, and Harry, and even Josephine has some money—but I support myself; I've never asked any of them for help. Although it is true that I could.

And then, not really aware that she had turned around, Eliza began in her mind to attack Kathleen.

What really bugged you was that your friends liked me; you can't stand that. You've always put down anyone I liked—

Miriam, and Harry, and even silly Peggy Kennerlie, who isn't worth not liking. Lena and Angie said they liked my poems and you hated that, and that's what's really wrong. You don't like it that I have any success. You'd be great if I were bleeding to death; you'd run right over with bandages. But you can't stand for anything good to happen to me. You're a foul-weather friend, Kathleen.

But, although what she was thinking may have been perfectly accurate, the weight of it—the obsessiveness—made Eliza almost sick. Why couldn't she simply let it go? Kathleen was a very hostile person; and their lives had outgrown each other.

Reason, unhappily, did not work as efficaciously as it should, and all those arguments, those unspoken but incredibly loud accusations and counteraccusations, continued for some time in Eliza's head, sometimes keeping her awake at night— until gradually, at last, they sounded like the dying echoes of shouts, in a hollow corridor.

Many months later, when Eliza's poem did, in fact, appear, her phone rang one day and an unfamiliar voice said, "Hi, this is Angie. I met you with Kathleen."

"Oh, of course, how are you?"

"Oh, fine. I just wanted to tell you that I was in the library the other day and there was the *Gotham*, with your poem—and it's so good, I really liked it."

Eliza was extremely pleased, both for good and for somewhat suspicious reasons—the latter, of course, having to do with Kathleen. They talked for a few minutes; Angie said that she was at work. "This week I'm a Kelly Girl. Jesus." They made some vague plans for getting together for coffee, or something.

Then, shyly awkward, Angie said, "I guess you haven't heard much from Kathleen."

"Uh—not really. No."

"Well, it got sort of bad, and so she moved out. This guy I know moved in—well, to be with me. I really like him, and he got along well with Jared, and Lena. And it was interesting, the idea of a man in a feminist group. He's a writer, I guess that's part of why he digs it. But everything worked except with Kathleen. She hated him; she was cross all the time, and cursing at us all."

With a kind of relief, Eliza laughed. "Well, that sounds like Kathleen," she said.

23 / "Watergate"

The first hint of something wrong in Washington affected Smith with the finality of a pronouncement of malignancy: suddenly all the symptoms made sense. Everything that had made him uncomfortable and suspicious (and that he had denied) fell into place. He hardly needed to listen to the rest, the revelations of espionage and lies, bribery, threats and pay-offs—of madness. And Smith felt his own illness, his spiritual malaise, to be terminal.

Like a very old person, he began to think with a sad persistence of a time in his life when he could have made a series of choices other than those he actually made, a time when many other paths were open and possible.

He remembered walking around Cambridge in his early teens, home on vacations from Groton, looking forward to Harvard. He even bought a green book bag from the Harvard Coop, hoping to be taken for a freshman (well, they were taking freshmen very young in those war years), hoping to be taken for anything rather than what he was: a prep-school boy on a desperately retained scholarship.

He planned that when he got to Harvard he would row on the crew, and he would study everything: history, literature, philosophy, anthropology. (He hadn't even heard of economics then.) And he would know (and love, and kiss!) a lot of girls, the marvelous available girls who clustered on the steps of Widener Library, in their baggy sweaters and pearls, loafers and white athletic socks. In those days his fantasies clung to small round blonds, blue-eyed, with the sort of skin that tans beautifully in the summer, on beaches at Ipswich and Duxbury.

Smith could see himself at fifteen or so, a tall dark serious, anxious boy, staring at those small blond girls (Eliza's type, actually) and at Widener itself, which surely contained all the knowledge in the world. Staring out at the Yard, bright with uniforms, with men in training for a virtuous war, a war already won.

Now, approaching middle-age, and heavy and wrong, Smith moved toward a visible depression. He rarely smiled, and he held his head down, bent as though his neck were permanently burdened.

Silent meals with Daria, who remained calm and observant, although, of course, very worried. "It's how he looked at college during finals," she told Eliza, on the phone. "Pale and desperate, sure he wouldn't get his *summa*. Now he's sure this country's had it, and in some crazy way he thinks it's all his fault."

"Daria, he's obviously in a depression. Shouldn't he see someone, or something? Really—" Eliza had just barely not said: You yourself should know.

"He won't see anyone. I think he had enough to do with shrinks over me."

Besides, Daria had certain half-formed theories of her own concerning sorrow. It should run its course, run all the way, she thought. In the meantime she was there for him (no more Reed); she remained quietly kind. Watching him, reading signs.

At Smith's request, the cook and maid had been let go (with large pensions); now once a week a silent and efficient man (a former hippie, now religious) came in to clean. Daria cooked and served their meals. Smith ate very little—a symptom that she understood. And, watching him, she learned something new, which was that the visual quality of food was most important to Smith: he ate what was attractive. She became an expert in the brightest and freshest vegetables and fruits, crispest salads, the whitest fish. (The ex-hippie approved of their diet.) She acquired a style of cooking that was somewhat Japanese, that was elegant and spare.

Smith conducted some business by mail; Daria would take the meticulously typed envelopes to the post office. She believed that they had less money than before; or was this message simply part of Smith's aura of depression? In any case, no matter: she had never known how much they had.

Smith wore rather ragged old shapeless sweaters, which Daria didn't know he had. And slippers, around the house. An old-young man.

Since, during those months, they did not see anyone except Eliza, it was not surprising that Reed had vanished from their life.

Within their several fenced-in acres, their compound, they would go for wet winter walks, not talking much (Smith always with his head down, neck bent to one side), among the guardian eucalyptus and poplars, cedars, elms.

At night they did not make love. Sex was the first thing to go—Daria knew that, and she knew, too, that Smith had never really liked it; he only drove himself, thinking that he should.

In the spring, instead of attempting suicide, Smith began to improve: appreciably, though not enormously.

Daria first noticed that he simply looked better, a little less pale and more alert. And then she saw that he had stopped looking at, listening to news. Fewer papers, unopened magazines. She was quiet about this, only saying, once, "We're not hearing the news tonight?" "No, it's getting dull. He'll resign next summer, that's obvious." Resign—the P.? But then she thought he was probably right.

Spring came beautifully that year; Daria and Smith went for drives and walks through the hills around Woodside, Los Altos, Palo Alto, Portola Valley—seeing blossoms everywhere, everything in bloom. Apple trees, plum and peach and apricot, and foaming yellow mimosa.

Desultorily, they talked about spring in New England, in their receding youth. "Remember driving out to Lexington and Concord? Yes. It comes on more violently there, don't you think? The brooks, and willows." And they said, "Funny, our being here in California." Becoming friends, almost intimates.

And having other, stranger conversations.

Smith said, "When you felt—*worst,* what was it like, the feeling? can you remember?"

Daria said, "It's hard to explain, but it was as though whatever separated me from anyone else no longer existed. I had no skin. I *was* everyone, everyone I saw, and if they were poor and miserable, I was." With a small sad laugh, she added, "I guess you could call it self-pity."

"No, that's not fair."

"Anyway, that's why I had to give everything away. It belonged to them, really."

Smith sighed, suddenly more isolated, because what she had described was so far from what he himself felt—how lonely to be unique. "You were probably right," he murmured, indistinct, wishing at that moment that he were Daria, were almost anyone else.

He was better, but not a great deal better.

He spent a lot of time listening to music. Handel, Bach.

Packages of books began to arrive at their house. Daria found them everywhere. (A new symptom was that Smith had become very messy, leaving things about, scattering ashes from his pipe.) Unwrapped, the books were bright and new, and they were all on history. Ancient, medieval. Nothing recent.

Smith said, "If you wanted to give some money now, who do you think you'd give it to?"

"Oh, I don't know, there're so many. Something called the National Council of Negro Women. I've always liked them; they feed children in Mississippi, other places. And CARE, Amnesty International."

Later he told her that he had sent checks to those groups—"quite a lot of money." But how much was a lot to Smith? Five hundred? A hundred thousand? Daria had no idea.

Smith was better.

Thinking less of him, being less concentrated on her husband, Daria now observed herself, and she noticed that something was wrong: she was eating less, she looked pale and dull. She was (again) memorizing numbers: 310 killed in a tornado; 100 feared dead in a motor-launch crash in Bangladesh; 250 dead, 500 missing in landslides in the Peruvian Andes; 107 killed in a Pan Am crash in Bali.

Had she "caught" Smith's depression, and translated it into her own familiar symptoms? Made his sadness her own?

Then it occurred to her to ask Smith for money to send to relief groups, the Committees in Aid of, the Red Cross. People coping with disasters.

"Of *course*," he said.

(Two hundred and fifty persons drowned: another motor launch capsized in a flooded river in Bangladesh.)

Daria thought, The P..was right about people like me. A

bleeding heart is exactly what I am; possibly bleeding to death.

(But then in August, when he resigned, she was even sorry for *him*.)

In September, Josephine, who was then in her middle sixties, had a stroke.

She was hospitalized in Portland, and then returned to her own house: not paralyzed, but weakened and depressed.

Daria and Smith heard this via phone calls from David White, Josephine's agent and friend. And then they talked to Josephine herself, who sounded as David described her, weakened and sad. But she was determined, nevertheless, to spend the winter there. "Really, it's a lot less strenuous than New York these days," she argued; and, less convincingly, "I'll be fine."

Eliza was occupied with Catherine and her children. Dylan, the oldest, had been diagnosed as having a malformed heart. Eliza said, "The terrible irony of it. I feel as though that poor child were being visited with my sins. Dear God, back to that hospital. Well, prick that he is, Gilbert Branner is still the best surgeon, I guess. And don't worry, it's the easiest defect to correct. He'll be fine. An ASD—I'll explain when I see you. Christ, I am sorry about poor Josephine."

"How would you feel," asked Smith, in a gentle and tentative way that had become his new manner, "about our spending the winter there with her, in Maine?"

Daria's heart gave a sudden leap upward at visions of snowdrifts, of snow floats out on the dark blue lake, and brilliant ice, and she said, "Smith, dear, I'd love to. That's perfect—you are good."

24 / Reed

In the following year, the year of Reed Ashford's fortieth birthday, in San Francisco spring never arrived at all. A cold dark winter became a cold and windy, foggy summer, with no intervening softer weather. Or sometimes there were a few bright blue hours, but those times served only to tease, to remind one of other Aprils and past delicately warm Mays and Junes.

In that prolonged and hardly bearable season, in Reed's romantically shingled Nob Hill cottage, everything leaked. Cold and wind penetrated his bones, so that waiting to be forty was even less pleasant than it normally would have been, for an exceptionally beautiful person.

Also, his teeth hurt. Or something in his mouth, maybe his gums, or his jaws themselves. Perhaps they were all rotting, would have to be removed? Sometimes he felt that waves of poison were rising from his teeth (gums, jaws) up to his very mind, as though all his thoughts were suffering from disease. Were poisoned.

Even in the bathroom mirror's brightest light, his hair looked dull. Not gray or white, just drab.

Still, he could sometimes smile at his own fears a little: loss of teeth, dulling of bright hair. Those were classics of middle age. Silly, even.

But what he recognized as dangerous, as no occasion for smiles, was an obsessive consciousness of dying, death; a strong tidal pull toward death, as though that were what he should do next. He *should* die. He should "take his own life." Once, he even found himself wondering what would become of his cats.

A bad series of thoughts; he knew that.

Then, one morning late in May, there was a sudden bright breakthrough of sunlight. Not really trusting it, Reed nevertheless pulled on his outdoor clothes, after feeding his new beautiful brown cats. He walked up the hill, up Nob Hill, to Huntington Park (to the corner where Daria first stood and thought of him with love). And he sensed instantly that he had made a mistake; he should not have come out. Everything was too bright for him: the brilliant shining Bay, the sleek cars rushing along Sacramento Street, the new green grass in the park. The blue sky hurt his eyes.

And then a familiar voice said, "Ah, Reed, how nice."

Eliza Quarles sat on a bench, her face uplifted to the sun. She looked rested, smooth-skinned, her clothes all clean and bright. Jeans, a pink sweater. Reed remembered that she was five years older than he; today she looked at least that much younger.

He sat down beside her and they discussed the weather. Would it ever get warm? Would spring come this year?

Once a love affair was over, Reed rarely thought of the woman involved; he almost forgot her, except for an occasional bad hour, usually late at night, drunk or stoned, when a parade of past loves would float by, a procession of lovely nameless ghosts. Sometimes, when he had been in love with Daria, he would think of Eliza, enjoying the slight perversity of their sisterhood. Lately he had not thought much even of Daria, having returned to his old pattern of much younger married girls, a few stray boys.

"I wrote to her because I thought her stuff was so terrific, and she turned out to be really nice," Eliza was saying.

Eliza was talking about poetry, women writers. Her new friends.

And why? he thought. Why tell me? He was so desperately bored with everything; how could he possibly hear about "meaningful work," or rewarding friends?

Eliza looked fully at him, and now Reed could see into her mind; she was thinking, How could I ever have loved this person, this completely vacuous man?

Deliberately he asked, "How's Daria?"

"Oh, how funny, I'd forgotten you had met her. She's fine—really well, I think." Making it clear that she had also forgotten meeting him, at Daria's house.

"Actually I met them both in Amsterdam, but it wasn't until much later that we fell in love with each other."

Eliza reddened and looked down, frowning. "In love? you and Daria?"

"Of course. For years. It just ended about a year and a half ago. She never told you?"

"No, of course not." She compressed her mouth in order not to say: And why did you have to tell me?

But they had both felt that unspoken sentence; too late, Reed was sorry.

A few minutes later, they got up from their bench; they managed to separate with a few polite words, and walked off in opposite directions.

Heading down Mason Street, northward, toward the Bridge, Reed thought that now would be the time. He could simply keep on walking in that direction, in the bright new fresh air, the valuable sunlight: a jaunty stroller, a youngish man in very good shape. (His teeth *looked* terrific.) There would be others walking on the bridge, couples, old people, tourists and joggers, and below would be the billowing white sails, blue waves. He would walk fast, smiling at everyone in a friendly recognition of such a rare day, its blessing. And then with a single gesture, a quick vault—off the bridge. Down, gone.

But how long is "down"?

And what about the cats?

He walked home, and in an hour or so it was raining again.

Some of Reed's friends knew vaguely that he had a birthday early in the summer, but no one knew on just what day, or on which year he arrived at important milestones. He hadn't talked about it, although the moment was on his mind: at 10:10 a.m. on June 4th, he would be forty years old.

And he did not know what to do about it. Give a party? Fly to New York (or Amsterdam) for the weekend with a terrific girl?

Jump off the bridge?

He was really too broke for gaudy trips or lavish parties (his business had been declining with a jarring speed; no one wanted to buy his expensive things); and besides, why should anyone know about his birthday? Instead, he invited a single friend, recently met, for dinner on the eve of his birthday, June 3rd: Alex Langlois, a nice and quite beautiful boy who was studying sculpture at the Art Institute.

He decided to make the dinner for two impressive. A little paté, a nice clear soup, crab curry with rice, a salad, a chocolate soufflé. Appropriate wines. The shopping for and preparation of all that fanciness would take up (would get him through) an entire day. A bad day: his last as a man in his thirties.

He enjoyed those hours, an entire afternoon of balmy sunshine. He shopped around in North Beach, on foot; he walked home and tidied up his house, and cooked, humming show tunes from his early youth as he worked: "So in Love" (a favorite of his mother's), "Wish You Were Here."

The phone rang just as he was finishing up. He walked toward it thinking, Good, I have just time for a short friendly chat, a little gossip, with whoever. Shall I say that it's my birthday?

"Hi, Ash?"

Ash? No one called him that. Stiffly he said hello.

"Ash, it's Alex. Look, man, I'm really sorry, but this chick I used to know in L.A. has shown up, and I thought you wouldn't mind. We could make it another night, okay? Well, *ciao*."

Reed hung up. He had mumbled something polite, and then he was stricken, overwhelmed with a heavier desolation than he could have imagined possible. Too late, he understood how much he had counted on Alex, that trivial pretty boy, to get him through the evening. Of course he could have asked a more reliable friend: some nice woman. And even now, desperately, it occurred to him to call someone: Rosalyn, Marge, Julia, Bobbie, Patricia. Daria, Eliza—the ghosts filed past the edges of his mind.

But there he was with all that fancy and perishable food, chilled wines and delicate spring flowers on the table. Impossible to sit down to all that alone.

Slowly, fastidiously, he began to push food down the disposal.

As always, at that ugly gurgling sound, the cats bounded out of the kitchen. And, watching their graceful leaps, Reed understood that he had been given a sign.

Of course: tonight. He didn't have to be forty at all, not ever. And at the phrasing of that thought he smiled twistedly. It was like a good joke that one couldn't tell.

He sat at the wooden kitchen table, sipping soup. Once everything was tidy, he began to imagine the Bridge. An exhilarating walk there, in the cold windy dark. Perhaps he could take a cab? Stupid to get mugged. A furtive climb over the barriers, an eluding run along the pedestrian walkway. The wet cold round steel railing.

Horrible, all of it. Reed shuddered, and then he thought, How preposterous; why should I spend even my last five minutes so miserably? Why not stay at home, comfortably drinking vodka and popping Valium?

He got up, and moved quickly from liquor pantry to bathroom shelf; he got both bottles, which he took into the bedroom. There he poured himself a good drink, and opened the pills. Then, picking up a pen, he wrote a note to his mail-carrier, a nice, rather fat young woman, who had always admired and coveted his cats.

His was the last stop on her route.

He told her to take the cats, and to call the police.

Odd that it had taken him so long to work this out.

25 / Eliza, Listening to Herself

"Do you remember meeting a man named Reed Ashford at our house? Did you read in the paper that he died? He killed himself."

Daria said those words rather factually over the telephone to Eliza; and Eliza, who had not yet read the paper that morning, or heard about Reed, began to tremble violently. She mumbled, "Yes, of course, I do remember him; that's too bad—" And she hung up as soon as she could, as though she were fearful that Daria could see her sitting there shuddering.

And *why?* Why those tremors, the cold rush through her veins? The last time she saw Reed, that day in Huntington Park, she had thought, How could I have ever loved him? Her one-summer lover, her sister's long-time love.

Or was he lying about Daria?

But Reed almost never lied; by nature he was a confessor, Eliza remembered. How, then, could Daria take it so calmly, with such apparent cool?

"Being in love with Reed wasn't real to me," Daria said, much later. "You know the way you sometimes feel at a party, looking around and wondering why you're there? I felt like that with Reed, a lot of the time. As though 'being in love' was a place I had to go through, on the way to somewhere else."

Which was not entirely unlike Eliza's own experience of Reed.

But Reed's death seemed to thrust Eliza back into a web of suicides. She thought first of the famous ones: Woolf, Plath. Marilyn, Billie. And then those frighteningly close to herself: her unknown father, Caleb Hamilton. Her husband, Evan Quarles.

And she was pursued by horrendously vivid moments of insight into some of those lives. She imagined Anne Sexton (in that instant she *was* Anne Sexton), back from lunch with a friend, thinking, perhaps tipsily, Well, why not now? Billie, shooting up in seedy hotels, with greedy, venal men. Marilyn, wild with anxiety, trying to phone someone, an important man, and not getting through; taking pills, losing count.

Evan, alone in his room in the old New England hotel, sleepless, thinking, I am queer. Drinking bourbon, taking pills.

Reed, growing old and less beautiful.

And she felt those people's sorrow, their despair; it poured through her veins like some dark dye, staining her blood and thickening in her heart. Their blind deathward surge became her own.

Suicide had caught up with her. Death.

Impossible to work. What she felt was all black and destructive.

Did that mean that she should—that she would die? It was not grief for Reed that she felt; it was sheer fear of death, her own private terror of suicide.

The weather of that summer was as unbearable as the contents of Eliza's mind, and at times she was unable to tell the difference between the long cold dark windy days, and the cold dark interior corridors of her brain. Still, she forced herself out into the weather. Every day she walked for at least a couple of hours: through the narrow packed streets and the good food smells of Chinatown, the elegant spaces of Nob Hill, Huntington Park (not knowing where Reed's house was, how near); sometimes out Union Street to a favorite bookstore; once into the Presidio, through those woods of wind-bent cypress, eucalyptus. In the cold, the heavy fog.

She talked to a relatively new friend, Jane, a novelist: one of the women writers whom Eliza had mentioned to Reed. Tall and lean, prematurely gray, with intense dark brown eyes, Jane had published three (good) novels and was struggling through a fourth. Eliza felt Jane to be almost her own opposite: Jane was more practical, more sensible, more *intelligent* than she was. Jane was not small and round. Jane had tall good-looking sons—twin sons—a talented and successful architect husband. Jane's life looked enviably stable, so that at times Eliza wondered, Should I have married someone (Harry?) and had more children? Should I perhaps be writing novels, not poetry?

To that last question, uttered by Eliza, Jane said, "Well, no. Maybe, but probably not." And then she laughed, still eying Eliza speculatively: "What I mean is you probably would have thought of a novel before, if that's what you wanted."

Eliza sighed. "No, you're right. I'm just tired of poetry. Everyone's, but especially mine."

Jane looked at her kindly, inquisitively. "Sometimes when I feel worst something good comes up out of it, some good work," she said. "A sort of phoenix syndrome. But you can't predict it."

"Everything seems to be lurching downward. Deathward," Eliza said.

Jane mused, "I think suicides scare everyone. Writers especially; so many of us have done it, after all."

After that conversation Eliza was somewhat less low, less preoccupied with darkness. She and Jane were not opposites, after all; they were both writers. And they had chosen each other as friends out of shared concern for that work. The friendship was not simply circumstantial, as several of Eliza's had been before—Peggy Kennerlie, the same college; Kathleen, an office friend—and as so many women's friendships often seemed to be.

In a morbid way, at night, she had been listening to Billie again: the most mournful, terrible songs, the dirges. "Strange Fruit," "Gloomy Sunday."

Now, with an effort, Eliza stopped doing that; she purposefully played Handel and Haydn, Mozart, Boccherini. And for variety she played old Beatle records, the silly cheerful ones from ten years back, when they only cared about being rich and famous and turning on with gorgeous birds.

At that time, midsummer, Smith and Daria were still in Maine with Josephine. Eliza had been getting curious letters from them all: letters about the strangely cold wet summer. (Something terrible is happening all over the world, Eliza thought.) Nothing about what any of them were really doing; specifically, why Daria and Smith were still there.

It was not for the sake of Josephine's health; everyone, even David, her kindly agent and friend, had written to Eliza that Josephine was fine, was very slightly weaker but still vigorous and alert. She swam when the days were warm enough; she went for long walks. She was writing.

And Daria said that Smith was well; he was not depressed any more.

Smith wrote that Daria had never seemed happier, or looked prettier. You dope, Eliza thought. Daria is not pretty; she's beautiful.

Aside from assessing each other's mental and physical well-being, what were they doing there?

Eliza had a sense that perhaps some precarious balance had

been struck between them all, and it occurred to her, of course, to go to see them. Christ, to see Maine! But she was prevented by a further sense that she would somehow throw them off; she would be the catalyst of change, of a new imbalance.

Instead, she drove north to see Catherine and her children: Dylan, whose operation was a success (surgeons, even other-wise-appalling men like Gilbert Branner, still have their uses, Eliza wryly thought), and the other two children—on their small Mendocino ranch, their farm. Jane had offered to lend her car, and then offered to go along, if that is what Eliza would like. And it was.

They drove north along the ordinary California highway: past shopping centers and subdivisions, motels and gas stations and restaurants. And past an occasional sloping yellow hill, with lovely dark spreading live-oak groves. Then they turned west-ward, off the main highway and onto a narrower, prettier road, through barren gray sheep country, past small country stores and gray beaten barns, wind-battered cypresses.

Catherine had no phone, of course, and so there was always some risk involved in a drive to see her; in rancid, nonmaternal moods, Eliza had sometimes wondered why she bothered.

This time the small white stucco house where Catherine and her children lived (an affront to the countryside) was boarded up. They turned in to the drive, which was simply a partially cleared space in an otherwise bare yard; they got out and walked slowly toward the house. A padlocked door, new pine planks nailed carefully over the windows. No message; nothing but absence could be read from that boarded house.

"You'd think—" Eliza began, and found that she was curiously near tears.

Jane agreed, "Yes, you certainly would."

"It's like some old movie, isn't it? Settlers swept off by Indians." Eliza gestured toward the bare yard.

"Except no one burned the house down. Everything left in pretty good shape."

"Well. Well, there's certainly no point in sticking around?"

"No, let's head back. We can stop somewhere for coffee, if you want."

In a slow, discouraged way, they got back into the car, slammed doors and headed out.

Jane drove toward the sea, the cold and gray forbidding Pacific, the great bearer of fog. Short sheer cliffs dropping straight down to the sea. No beaches, and nowhere any look of summer. A gray cold seasonless desolation everywhere.

Instead of crying, Eliza began to talk, in an extended burst.

"*Catherine.* Whatever does go on in her mind, I've never known at all. She's a sort of willfully passive person. People talk her into things, and then she overdoes them. She could have twenty children before she's through. Or join the Hari Krishnas, or Reverend Moon. Or she could be a real pioneer, somewhere, if there were a frontier. She's really a throwback, a kind of woman that none of the rest of us ever were. I often feel that I can't appreciate Catherine because we're so unlike. I wonder if Josephine ever felt something like that about me, except that we aren't all that different, only the way we look. 'Literary women,' God, how tiresome. You know, there's a sense in which I don't *like* Catherine, and it feels very much like Josephine's not liking me. What is this? Don't mothers and daughters like each other? Is it terribly different with boys?"

Jane frowned, concentrating on those questions. "I guess, a little. But I really don't know."

"This is so irrational. I'm behaving as though Catherine knew I was coming and deliberately boarded up the house to greet me."

"That's not so irrational. She did know that eventually you'd come up."

. . .

But irrational was exactly how Eliza continued to feel, over the next few dark cold weeks of late July and early August.

Not writing at all, barely able to concentrate on reading a book (magazines were better), she recognized danger, and she took certain steps. She spent a lot of time waxing furniture, and she continued to walk a lot (and considered, and discarded, the notion of smoking again).

But, walking, she recognized that some claustrophobic pull was keeping her close to home. She walked, but never to those outlying parts of the city that she had once enjoyed. She walked around Russian Hill and neighboring North Beach, her limits. One day she found herself walking all around the park, Washington Square, around it once, and then again. Around the beautifully sloping green space, past the stands of eucalyptus. And she became aware of a great sadness in what she was seeing, and of an emptiness in herself: she was as bare, as bleak, as the park.

Then she thought, Of course, ten years ago this is where all the hippies came and lay around in the sun, in their bright mad clothes, with their guitars and dogs and chunky little children.

She understood that she was staying close to home because Catherine might show up.

There was no word from Catherine.

There was no word, in fact, from anyone, until one afternoon there was a call from Harry. He was flying up in half an hour; he had to meet someone for a drink, but could he and Eliza meet for dinner? Would it be okay if he stayed with her? And he named a restaurant to which she had not been, although it was within blocks of her house. It faced the park she has been walking around, again and again. Washington Square.

Yes, of course she would meet him for dinner; of course he could stay. (The terms of their relationship were delicate: were she to any extent involved with anyone else, she could have said no, and that would have been all right. Or, supposedly, it would have been all right; so far, she had never said no to Harry.)

But, changing the bedsheets, then getting into her bath, Eliza was aware of a terrible difference between this present moment, her present feelings, and how she usually felt, and had felt for years, anticipating Harry.

Now, in the tub, she looked down at her large wet pale body, big floating breasts and round stomach, dark rising pubic hairs, and hugely foreshortened legs. Gross, pallid jelly—a jellyfish of a body, it seemed to her.

She did not want *at all* to make love.

Which was not to say that she had always, at every moment, wanted to before; of course not. But simply that she usually had, more often than not; she had almost always wanted Harry. What she had never felt was this negative, this *no* to sex.

It was terrible, and frightening. Age? A somewhat early menopause?

Dressed, and downstairs in her kitchen, she made herself a strong drink (also out of character for her) before going to meet Harry.

Half a block from the restaurant, she was almost overcome with what felt like shyness: *could* she open the door and go in and look around for Harry?

She did, of course, and he was there at the bar, mere feet away from her. Harry, smiling welcome, saying her name. They kissed, with great affection. Affection for Harry almost made Eliza cry, which was another new fear of hers: a burst of tears.

They were given a cozy window table, looking out to the park; through immensely thick old Lombardy poplars they glimpsed the neon lights of Columbus Avenue.

Harry had begun to look older, she noticed in the lamplight as he spoke to the waiter, ordering drinks. His bony nose was yet more prominent, and his blue eyes were paler, although still incredibly intense. The most *living* eyes in the world, Eliza thought, and again experienced an awful urge to cry.

Turning now fully to her, Harry said, "My God, it's so

good to see you. I've been so tired, and that last flop was no fun for a man of my years. I've got some ideas, and then at other times, you know, I feel absolutely depleted. I think I've told every story I know."

"I know: I've said all the poems in my head. Harry, we're getting old!"

Ruefully they both laughed, thus pushing that moment away.

He said, "You're a lovely old lady, Eliza."

She told him about Catherine, managing, she was pleased to note, to sound considerably less worried than she was.

Dinner came, which turned out to be good.

But sometime later, in the midst of what was becoming a much better evening than she had thought possible, Eliza had a sudden and insistent sense of death, of the presence of death. Looking out through the heavy ancient poplars, out to the lights, she imagined death; and she *saw* herself sitting there, thinking of death.

And she thought again of not wanting to make love; herself dry and old, opposed to sex. Obsessed with death—dry—old.

They walked the several blocks back to Eliza's house, leaning against the marauding wind, the cold relentless fog.

Even inside it was cold. Harry made a small fire, and Eliza went to make coffee, to get out brandy.

And almost immediately the telephone rang.

Not Catherine; it was Daria, from Maine.

"Eliza, I've been trying to get you—it's Josephine. Another stroke. No, really not a bad one. The doctor says that if you come right away you'll just scare her; he's sure—he's sure she'll be okay. But could you come in a few days? And in the meantime of course I'll call you a lot—"

Eliza went back into the living room, where, in Harry's arms, she was overtaken by the long-threatening tears, the sobs that went on and on. "It's horrible!" she cried out. "I was right.

This feeling I've had of death. And you know, I've never told you this—nor, God knows, anyone: when Josephine had her first stroke, the first thing I thought was I'm safe from her now. You see? So she had to have another one."

Harry gave the gentlest possible laugh. "Baby, darling, come on. *You* forced Josephine to have another stroke? Really, powerful in your own way as you are, I just can't buy it."

"But what a terrible thing to think, after a stroke—"

"Look, read a few old plays. You're not exactly the first person who'd find a crippled parent easier to deal with than a powerful one."

Eliza had only been half listening; everything that he said would make much more sense later on.

"Catherine," she said, in the same vein. "For all I know, Catherine could be dead."

"Baby, come on. Catherine is just careless, inconsiderate. Not dead."

"And I can't write any more. That's dead, too."

Later it was Harry who made their coffee, and then they went up to bed. They did not make love.

26 / *A House, a Lake and Islands*

And so, after years of talking about it, of plans and delays and postponements, Harry and Eliza went to Maine. They flew to Boston where they rented a car (a small Ford, not quite up to Harry's usual standards: the Seventies had had their effect) and they headed north, up the turnpike.

Past Portland, they turned off onto smaller roads, and it all began to look overpoweringly familiar to Eliza: the stone-fenced fields, the dark woods laced with birches, the barns and houses, crossroads stores and small libraries.

On the last tarred road, before turning off onto their own private stretch, there was a succession of similar hills, each cresting to a view of fields and woods and farther hills; until from the last one there was, suddenly, the lake! Eliza, at that view, as all her life she had, cried out in triumph (forgetting all that death), "There—there it is—the lake!"

A large bright blue lake, into which long points of land extended. And there were small dark irregularly shaped islands; one long island that was the shape of a fish.

From there on everything was known by heart: the turn onto a narrow white road, between just yellowing fields; another turn, uphill and through some leafy woods. A gray farmhouse (much larger than its barn) abandoned now, stark and tall above a bare gray yard. More fields, stone-fenced, edged with pine and hemlock, and then the road entered a darker stretch of woods, between huge black trunks of Norway pines. Solemn, a cathedral silence.

Then another lighter, leafier wood, another turn: the orchard (theirs) with small gnarled gray trunks and gray-green leaves. Stone fences. Indian paintbrush, goldenrod.

A driveway, lawn and long low-lying house. The long porch, porte-cochère, the parking area. Cars were there, but no one was in sight. They parked and got out, bringing bags, and Harry said, "My God, it's the greatest house I've ever seen. Eliza, love, it's marvelous. And the lake—*Why* haven't we come before?"

They were expected; the front door had been left open. They left their bags in the hall and then went down the steps to the path across the lawn, to the beach. The lake: blue water, lightly lapping at the sand.

They walked along a seemingly empty beach; they came to a familiar rock, high and gray and oddly slanted, and there, on the other side of it, were an unfamiliar (unfamiliar together) couple: Josephine and Smith. Both white-haired, both, in their separate ways, distinguished.

Greetings, kisses, introductions. Smith was now standing, and Eliza knelt on the sand beside her mother, who looked—all right: somewhat more frail, a little tired, but her eyes were as blue and bright as ever; as lively as the lake. An old, but not a dying woman. (But no longer dangerous.)

In almost her old emphatic voice, Josephine said, "*Well.* It's really marvelous that you're here."

And, a little after that, after the perfection of that August day had been remarked upon, Eliza asked, reasonably enough, "Where's Daria?"

Josephine and Smith looked at each other, and Eliza was

again struck by their air of being a couple, in whatever (surely not sexual) sense. Josephine said, simply, "We don't know. She left the day before yesterday."

Two days ago, at breakfast, as she read the paper, Daria had begun to cry; they were not sure about what, but given the news it could have been anything—deaths by plagues and starvation, floods, the homeless, the hopelessly ill. Josephine and Smith did not say that it was like Daria ten years ago; they didn't have to. She got up, and said that she was going for a walk, and did not come back. They did not know where she was. They were frightened, but at this point calling the police seemed somehow an invasion of her privacy; they both believed that somehow, somewhere, Daria knew what she was doing.

As Eliza did, although, like them, she was frightened. She stood up, and not quite knowing what she meant to do, she said to them, "Don't worry. I'll find her."

With Harry (of whom, at this moment, she was almost unconscious), she walked slowly back toward the house, across the lawn, up steps, across the porch. Inside the house, at the foot of the stairs, Harry started to go up with their bags, but Eliza said, "You go on up. Our rooms are the ones at the end of the hall. I'll be a minute."

"Okay. I need a shower."

Eliza turned back to the still-open front door; she went out and sat on the porch, in one of the wicker chairs, as though she had a plan. She looked out blankly at the bright, bright lake, thinking desperately of her sister. Of Daria.

Eliza could see her: thick-lashed, yellow-eyed, with tawny skin.

She saw a very young Daria, in a trim gray flannel coat, who had come up to see her older married sister, and who for the first time in her life was staying alone in a hotel. (While Evan was teaching at Raleigh, a month or so before his suicide in that same hotel.) Daria was saying, "This is the most wonderful place I've ever been! Did you see the floorboards in the hall? They're so *uneven*, it's wonderful—it's like being on a boat."

The Ark was the name of that hotel, the place that young Daria loved.

Eliza had no other ideas, and this was no crazier than doing nothing at all.

But what name would Daria use? Worthington— Paulus—Hamilton?

When, finally, she got the desk of The Ark on the phone, Eliza said that she was looking for three friends who might be staying there, and she gave those names.

A long creaking pause, and then, "No, Miss, I'm sorry, we've got none of them here." The finality of New Hampshire vowels.

Eliza's heart fell, although she knew that what she was doing was crazy. She thanked the voice on the other end, and was about to hang up, when on a probably crazier impulse she said, "How about Erskine? Do you have a Daria Erskine?" Josephine's maiden name: Josephine Erskine Hamilton; Eliza Erskine Hamilton Quarles; Daria Erskine Paulus Worthington.

"Yep. Miss Erskine just now came in. I'll ring her room." Two trilling rings.

Daria said, "Eliza, how *did* you—?"

"By magic. Divination. No help from you, God knows."

"*Eliza*—" Daria began to explain. "I was sitting there feeling so unhappy, as though I weighed five hundred pounds, so heavy and so miserable that I could never move again. And then in the midst of it, all that crying and helplessness, I saw that I had to do something, almost anything but just sit there and cry—I'd been doing that for years. And so I walked into town, and there was a bus just stopped at the crossroads, with 'Raleigh' on the front of it. Oh, you're right; I know it was bad to do, to worry everyone. But I only meant to walk into town. It was seeing that name on the bus, and remembering the place.

But, Eliza, it worked, my mind cleared. I've got an idea."

"Well—good."

"Look, I'm just two hours away, and there's a bus at four. Would you ask Smith to meet me? I want to talk to him first."

Eliza returned to the beach, to Smith and Josephine and Harry, and told what had happened, how she had found Daria. She had an uneasy sense of being praised overmuch for something that was easy. Sometimes, she had even had that feeling about a poem: anyone could have written down those particular words, in that order. She said, "I just called her. It just came to me where she would be. After all, it's quite near, and I knew she liked it there."

Early that evening—Smith had gone to meet Daria; presumably they would stop and talk for a while—the phone rang and Eliza, somehow prewarned, rushed to answer it. And it was Catherine, calling collect, from Boston.

Very tired, tired beyond anger (tired of Catherine?), Eliza said, "Well—well, of course I've been worried. What do you think?"

"You didn't get my cards?"

"Cards? No, I didn't."

"I'm sure I sent them." Long explanations followed: Catherine and the three kids and these new friends were going up to Canada to stay with some neat friends. Farms, animals, self-sufficiency. Listening, Eliza experienced an unfamiliar, at first not recognized reaction: she was bored. Bored, tired and beginning to be relieved; she was beginning to see that she had done all she could for Catherine, over the past twenty-five years. Some other time, with Catherine in some other phase (she hoped, and it was quite possible), they could have a new relationship, but all the old mother-anxiety was over now.

Catherine would have to attend to herself, as Eliza would.

At the end of the explanations, Eliza simply asked, "How long will you be in Boston?"

"Oh, a couple of weeks. We have to sort of get things together here. Why? Are you coming down?"

"No." No, Catherine, I'm not. "Look, give me your number, where you are. I'll call you tomorrow, okay?"

Later, out on the porch with drinks, in their adjacent chairs, Harry and Eliza regarded the silent lake in the clear and cooling August evening air. Eliza was thinking of the bottom of the lake, in the shallow waters, where she used to see ripples in the sand, ripples shaped like delicate human ribs, like skeletons. And then thinking of the deepest parts of the lake, observed from a canoe, in which giant, rounded, possibly Ice Age boulders were terrifyingly visible. She was thinking of those darkest depths of the lake. Of drowning there, among rocks and small translucent fish. It would seem an easy—a familiar death, she thought exhaustedly.

Harry was thinking of a movie he would like to make, to be filmed, at last, in Mexico. In Ixtapanejo.

But for the past few days, the days since Daria's phone call from Maine to San Francisco, about Josephine's stroke, they had not made love. Had hardly talked, in fact.

Was it over, then, their remarkable friendship–sexual rapport?

They both wondered that.

Driving to meet Daria, at the crossroads from which she left—driving over those roads that by now are familiar to him, Smith thought of when he had come here first, of the drive with Josephine. (Was Catherine, then a small child, in the back seat that day? He believed she was, but couldn't remember. Josephine's obvious attempts to draw him out; his resistance, and his strange thought: If you really knew me, if I let you know me, you would stop this marriage. But what could he have meant by that? He loved Daria, he wanted her for his wife.

Then, as now, late August. Goldenrod and a few bright maple leaves. Brilliant sharp blue glimpses of the lake. Smells of grass, and wind, and sweetly rotting apples.

Smith was almost surprised to see her, standing there where she was supposed to be, the bus having come and gone somewhat ahead of schedule. A thin dark-haired young woman in dusty jeans and a clean, unironed yellow cotton shirt. Beautiful, really, with a nervous, elegant walk, in spite of those clothes.

She got into the car and leaned to kiss him, in the brushing way that they had kissed for years, parting or greeting each other. Smith noticed that despite the jeans she looked very clean: scrubbed and tired, eager-looking, *young*. The sight of her made him tired.

She said, "I'm sorry, really. I do know that was childish, running away. But it just came to me—I sort of had to. And I did think a lot. Smith, how much money do I have?"

"Money?" He fussed at starting up the car. And although it was Daria, his wife, who had asked this, Smith automatically resisted; in his world large sums of money were vaguely referred to, never explicitly named. "A bundle" was the phrase his people (the Money People) currently used, which could mean anything at all.

Daria had a lot of money in her own name, a big bundle, but why should she want to know just how much?

And he was quite right to resist.

"Let's stop here," she said as they reached the small meadow just past the forest of Norway pines.

They stopped, parked, and she told him that she wanted to get a job, in Boston, or probably Cambridge, maybe just a volunteer job, but with people she liked: "You know, my kind.

Do-gooders, bleeding hearts, some do-good organization." She said that hurriedly, breathily. And then she said that she wanted to give away all her money.

Smith was forced—partly from sheer fatigue in the face of so much energy—to take her seriously, although many of his instincts were outraged. She—Daria was outrageous. But still she was a person, with rights. Smith believes in justice. And the money was indeed her own. He gave it to her.

Daria had, in her own name, about a million dollars.

Her eyes grew wide as he named the sum—warm yellow eyes; so much money to give away. And her voice was high, quite childlike. "But, Smith, that's wonderful, how wonderful of you, to make so much money. I can't wait to give it all—"

Smith then said NO, so firmly that she listened. He said, "It would be much better for you to keep the money and distribute the income every year. Look, suppose you give one of your favorites—United Farm Workers?—say, five hundred grand. They'd have to invest it—choose a counselor, some-one, pay for advice. My point is I really think I'm better at that than their person would be. You know I'm great at making money. Let me handle the money for you."

Daria was convinced, although it would have been more fun to give away huge sums than the income from huge sums. However, she could admit to herself that this was a little infantile, grandstandish. Smith sounded right.

He further explained about I.R.S. rulings on contribu-tions, et cetera; it all made sense.

In a curious way, Daria and Smith became business partners, of a somewhat original sort.

Daria said to Smith, "We'd better get on to the house, don't you think? Josephine—dinner—"

Smith was experiencing strange physical sensations: a dizziness amounting to nausea. Was this a heart attack? Or madness? He managed to start the car, to drive over the remaining mile or so of the narrow white road, to the orchard, to the house, without letting Daria know that anything was wrong. Whatever it was, it gradually passed.

At dinner, Josephine, in her old flounced and flowery dress, talked almost incessantly, as she did when she was nervous. She said, in part, "I don't know why, it must be loss of recent memory, but lately I've thought so much of Franz, the summer we spent up here, when you were a baby, Eliza. He was my second husband, who died in the civil war in Spain," she explained to Smith, who probably knew this already. And then to Eliza: "Your Harry looks remarkably like Franz. The same deep face lines."

Having been told in a general way of Daria's plans, Eliza suddenly thought, Catherine will leave Dylan in Boston with Daria. This sentence or prophecy flashed across her mind, and she further thought, Daria has always wanted to have Dylan; she will take an apartment for the two of them, and send Dylan to Shady Hill or some other good school there, in Cambridge or in Boston. A "good school" will be the excuse between her and Catherine for Catherine's leaving him there. The real reason being that Daria wants him more, and it will probably be better for him with Daria.

"Do you realize that Daria and I were married just fifteen years ago tomorrow?"

This sentence was spoken quietly by Smith to Eliza. Daria had gone to bed, and Harry and Josephine were inside, talking. Like dancers, these two strange couples had momentarily shifted partners. Eliza and Smith were walking along the beach, alone, in the cooling night.

Smith's words seemed to explode within her head, and she

was ricocheted back to that moment when she and Smith were sitting on the porch, and Smith was saying—what?—and she was imagining Billie. She saw the lake as it was then, and now: the heavy waning moon and its glittering path.

Then she looked out to the beach where she had meant to walk, where now, on the cold coarse damp sand, she walked with Smith.

He was saying something even more startling, though still in his rather proper, quiet voice: "Why didn't you stop us, Eliza? You must have seen something. Christ, if only I could have married someone like you."

"But Smith—" She had begun to say: You're crazy, or—we don't even like each other. And had realized that neither of these things was true, or was no longer true.

"You must think I sound nuts," he said, with a tiny laugh.

"No, but I always thought you thought I was."

Somewhat self-consciously they both laughed at that as, seemingly an echo, a loon called from somewhere out in the rocky islands.

Partly to change their mood, and also because for years she had wanted to know (for five years, since her birthday in Ixtapanejo), Eliza asked, "Who were you talking to in Washington—all those calls, during—those years?"

"Oh, no one, a girl. A reporter. She looked a little like you." This curious last an afterthought.

Later he said, "Daria doesn't want a divorce, although she doesn't *not* want one, but I think we should. I like to have things clear; you know how I am."

I do? Eliza asked, "Shouldn't you tell her that?" This conversation with Smith was beginning to sound as crazy as their first, when he talked about appropriate places to live.

With the most terrible sadness, he said, "It's too late, isn't it? I made all the wrong choices too early."

Not entirely sure what he meant (political or sexual choices—possibly both?), Eliza did what she had vaguely thought of doing, fifteen years back: she stopped walking and she grasped Smith's arm; she leaned upward, on tiptoe, and most gently kissed his mouth, finding it as smooth and soft as she had imagined.

She said, "I really like you, Smith."

With one hand he pressed her shoulder, saying nothing.

The next day no one mentioned a wedding anniversary.

A few days later, Josephine and Smith and Daria decided to go to the beach—the Atlantic coast, a few hours away. Harry and Eliza stayed at home. To Josephine, Harry said, "I can't bear to leave this house, and we have to get back to California in a couple of days."

Having made love lengthily the night before, and quickly again in the morning (whatever was wrong suddenly, miraculously healed), they were warm and comfortable and friendly with each other. I like Harry more than anyone, Eliza thought for the hundredth time.

It was a lovely day for them; they spent most of it on the beach, near the edge of the water, the dark blue lake beneath a brilliant deep blue sky; an early fall sky, although the day was warm.

And, in a desultory way, as they did and had always done on beaches, Eliza and Harry were making a movie, talking about it; perhaps they would make it together.

"Well, there's always the stewardess," Harry said.

The stewardess movie was one that they had half drunkenly—or sometimes when they were high—invented over the years: the girl with a man in every port, in Rome and Athens and Paris and Amsterdam. They had cast and recast it many times, and it was at least fairly funny every time.

But now Eliza had a new idea. "What about Daria?" she asked.

"Daria?"

"I think she's a kind of heroine."

"Maybe." Harry frowned, not really listening to this idea.

"And you could have beautiful shots of Daria and Reed in Amsterdam."

"Really? Did that happen?"

"Yes, I think so. He told me, and then I began to think, Once they were there at the same time. In any case, it's where they met."

Harry took this in, or tried to. "The poor bastard," he finally said. "But how fantastic they must have looked together."

"Yes, *exactly.*" And behind her eyes Eliza was seeing just that scene: Daria and Reed in Amsterdam, on a terrace that overlooked a dark canal. Lights dancing in the water.

A small wind had come up, just enough to deepen the ripples in the lake, to ruffle the birch leaves in the clumps of trees on the drying lawn. And with a curious premonition of loss Eliza turned to look at the house: the long low-lying structure so settled onto its land, among the dark familiar trees. The long porch, old wicker chairs and suspended swing.

After this winter here, Eliza thought (she knew) that Josephine would decide that, finally, it was time to sell the place. And Smith would agree; he would advise her sensibly. Daria will say that she doesn't want to own the house—as I will, Eliza thought.

For a moment against those thoughts she closed her eyes, and in the dark space behind her vision she saw, or suddenly felt, an urgency of words, a kaleidoscope that stopped to form a pattern. Words, her own work. But stronger, somehow enlarged.

When she opened her eyes and turned to Harry, she was smiling, almost breathless from an excitement in her chest. But she only said, "I'll be glad to get back."

"Me, too. It's time for me to do some work." And then he said, "Shall we make a bargain? Both work our heads off this fall and if it goes well, if I can feel a hit coming, we'll go to Mexico. Ixtapanejo in January?"

"Well, okay, if mine goes well, too." But she was not thinking about Ixtapanejo, or, really, about Harry.

Rather solemnly they shook hands, before they kissed.

And then Eliza said, "How odd: I've just remembered—today's my birthday."

"*Well.*"

Well.

ACKNOWLEDGMENTS

Portions of this book originally appeared in *The Atlantic Monthly*, *The Paris Review*, and *Redbook*.

Grateful acknowledgment is made to the following for permission to reprint previously published material:

Chappell & Co., Inc. (New York): For use of lyrics from "Now They Call It Swing" by Hirsch, Deleath, Cootier, and Handman. Copyright 1938 by Santly Bros.–Joy, Inc. Copyright renewed, assigned to Chappell & Co., Inc. International copyright secured. All rights reserved. Used by permission.

Famous Music Corporation: For use of lyrics from "Blue Orchids" by Hoagy Carmichael. Copyright 1939 by Famous Music Corporation. Copyright © renewed Famous Music Corporation, 1966.

Chappell & Co. Ltd (United Kingdom): For use of lyrics from "I Cover the Waterfront" by John W. Green and Edward Heyman. Copyright 1933 by Harms Inc. Reproduced by kind permission of Victoria Music Publishing Co. Ltd (Chappell & Co. Ltd).

Warner Bros. Inc.: For use of lyrics from "I Cover the Waterfront" by John W. Green and Edward Heyman. Copyright 1933 by Warner Bros. Inc. Copyright renewed. All rights reserved. Used by permission.

Chappell & Co. Ltd (United Kingdom): For use of lyrics from "I Gotta Right to Sing the Blues," music by Harold Arlen, words by Ted Koehler. Copyright 1932 by Harms Inc. (Warner Bros.). Reproduced by kind permission of Chappell & Co. Ltd.

Warner Bros. Inc.: For use of lyrics "I Gotta Right to Sing the Blues," music by Harold Arlen, words by Ted Koehler. Copyright 1932 by Warner Bros. Inc. Copyright renewed. All rights reserved. Used by permission.